DIPLOMATIC BAGGAGE

Recent Titles by James Melville

THE BODY WORE BROCADE
THE BOGUS BUDDHA
HAIKU FOR HANAE
RELUCTANT RONIN

DIPLOMATIC BAGGAGE

James Melville

WEST LOTHIAN DISTRICT COUNCIL
DEPARTMENT OF LIBRARIES

This first world edition published in Great Britain 1994 by
SEVERN HOUSE PUBLISHERS LTD of
9–15 High Street, Sutton, Surrey SM1 1DF.
First published in the USA 1994 by
SEVERN HOUSE PUBLISHERS INC., of
425 Park Avenue, New York, NY 10022.

Copyright © 1994 by James Melville

All rights reserved.
The moral rights of the author have been asserted.

British Library Cataloguing in Publication Data

A CIP record for this title is held at the British Library

ISBN 0 7278 4717 1

All situations in this publication are fictitious and
any resemblance to living persons is purely coincidental.

Typeset by Hewer Text Composition Services, Edinburgh.
Printed and bound in Great Britain by
Hartnolls Ltd, Bodmin, Cornwall.

To John Blackwell
with gratitude and respect

Author's Note

It is a matter of record that as a British Council officer I served as Cultural Attaché in the British Embassy in Budapest in 1972 and 1973, ten years before the time in which my alter ego James Melville has set the fantasy which follows. For fantasy it is, though I have inevitably drawn on my personal memory bank for some of the details which embellish it. It is therefore probably more important than usual to stress that none of the characters depicted are based on living persons.

The written Hungarian language has many accents, but I have not used them in the fragments of dialogue or place-names which occur in this book, on the grounds that they would have been an unnecessary complication for most readers, while those who do know the language have no need for indications as to its pronunciation.

Principal Characters

Ben Lazenby	Cultural Attaché, British Embassy, Budapest
Tom Dalby	His counterpart in Bucharest
"Loo Brush"	Lazenby's Head of Chancery
Gosta Lundin	Finnish journalist
Emma Jarvis	Lecturer in English, Debrecen University
Viktor Szekacs	Desk officer, Institute of Cultural Relations (KKI)
Comrade Nagy	AVH (Hungarian security service) officer, attached to KKI
Ferencz Molnar	Gipsy activist
Agnes	Gipsy child
Sandor	Agnes's younger brother
Svetlana Ivanova	Deputy Resident, KGB, Budapest
Col. Pavel Galitsin	Assistant Military Attaché, Soviet Embassy, Budapest
Maj. Grigory Vishinski	Col. Galitsin's cousin
"Boris"	Bulgarian truck driver
"Ivan"	The same
Lt. Enescu	Romanian police officer
Lajos Ranki	Hungarian customs official
Sgt. Miklos Hunyadi	Hungarian police officer

Prologue

April 1982

It was very quiet, and Lazenby could hear the ticking from the cooling engine of the Rover on the other side of the road as, his heart pounding, he approached the huge vehicle and surveyed it, going first to its rear. The seals were intact. He then walked round to the front. In the gloom and at close quarters the massive flank looked as formidably forbidding as a sheer cliff face, and when Lazenby reached the cab he saw that its side window was well above his head. He remembered during the drive from Bucharest seeing how easily the Bulgarian drivers clambered into their cabs; but they were used to it and he wasn't.

As quietly as possible he put his right foot in the metal bracket that provided the lowest step, grasped the hand grip and hauled himself off the ground, searching with his left for the recess he'd seen about eighteen inches higher. After a few fumbled tries he found it and pulled himself up so that he could peer through the window. His arms and legs were aching and he was giving himself a crick in the neck, but he hung there indecisively for nearly a minute longer before groping for the handle of the door and trying it.

It yielded at once and the door began to swing open, very nearly dislodging Lazenby from his perch. Saving himself in the nick of time he awkwardly swung himself into the cab and sat in the driver's seat, easing his protesting muscles, feeling a little sick, and asking himself how in the world a routine interview in London just over a year before could have led to the alarming situation in which he now found himself: exhausted, frighteningly responsible for the woman in the Rover across the road, and most certainly the target of two East European security services.

What he had been told in London that afternoon in March 1981 had come as such an interesting surprise . . .

"Budapest, eh?" To give himself time to assimilate what the Director of Personnel had been saying to him, Ben Lazenby nodded several times. "In Hungary," he then murmured thoughtfully.

The Director smiled sourly. "By crikey, no flies on you, Ben, are there? Now listen, this proposed posting is not only highly confidential, but entirely provisional. All manner of hoops to be gone through before you can breathe a word, even to your nearest and dearest." He clapped a hand to his mouth and then shrugged apologetically. "Sorry, Ben, forgot for a moment your divorce has just come through."

"Oh, that's okay. What sort of hoops?"

The Director indicated Lazenby's red "Restricted Circulation" personal file which lay before him. "Well, for a start, I see you've never been positively vetted. It hasn't been required for your previous postings, but you'd have diplomatic status in Hungary. Haven't got any guilty secrets, have you?"

"Hasn't everyone? Yes, of course I have, but no more than you, I should think."

"Ah. Quite so. Yes, well, it'll be a month or two before we can get you cleared, so don't go blabbing about this posting to *a soul*, understand? Besides, there's an even more important reason. Once you've been PV'd, the Foreign Office has to ask the Hungarians for their agreement to accept you before we can go public. East Europeans get frightfully shirty if they get the idea that they're merely being asked to rubber-stamp a *fait accompli*."

"You can't rubber-stamp a *fait accompli*", Lazenby pointed out, earning himself an even sourer smile. "Anyway, I'll keep it to myself, I promise. So nobody else here's in the picture?"

"Nobody *at all* outside the higher reaches of Personnel, and it must stay that way. I take it you're pleased? Especially as it'll mean promotion?"

"I haven't really taken it in yet, but yes, I think so. Thank you."

"Splendid. And remember, keep absolutely mum."

In something of a daze, Lazenby made his way back to the desk one floor below in the building tucked snugly between Admiralty Arch and Trafalgar Square, at which he currently laboured as deputy to the director of a department concerned with overseas students.

To be a bachelor again after ten years of marriage, thirty-eight, physically fit, tolerably presentable and childless to boot, was in itself a reason for mild euphoria, now that he had overcome the initial pain, learned to live with his regrets and recovered some self-esteem. He had no doubt done his share in bringing about the failure of the marriage, and probably deserved to lose Susan. Yet after all it was she who had ditched him in the end, in favour of a rising and, in Lazenby's own view, obnoxious young barrister who hoped to become a Tory parliamentary candidate.

Hence her urgent desire for an uncontentious divorce: for Giles (he *would* be called Giles) wanted to be able to present himself before constituency selection committees in a respectably married state. Susan had during Lazenby's stint at headquarters acquired a well-paid job in public relations, and she made no financial demands, explaining complacently that Giles's career prospects were in an altogether bigger league than Ben's. He therefore kept the modest flat in Fulham that had been their London base during their two spells overseas and most of its contents.

When Lazenby applied to join the British Council's overseas service back in the early seventies he had been motivated primarily by a desire to see the world and to earn a comfortable salary while doing so; and secondarily by a naive pride in British cultural achievements and an idealistic conviction that foreigners had something to learn from them. The former consideration had over the subsequent ten years or so proved to be more durable than the latter, but Lazenby's flippant manner concealed the vestiges of a missionary spirit.

The prospect of working overseas again, and on promotion to Grade D with generous allowances, cheered him more and more as it sank in. He hummed tunelessly as he paused at the vending machine and bought a plastic beaker of the hot chocolate which was the only one of the beverages available that was half-way drinkable, and carried it with him to what senior management, ever trying to catch up with the latest jargon, encouraged him without success to think of as his "work station". His nearest colleague, a nice woman called Jenny, was leaning over and speaking into his telephone.

"Hang on a sec," she said as she spotted him. "For lo and behold, he is nigh." Jenny and her husband were members of the Sealed Knot, and spent their weekends re-enacting historic battles. She was rather given to the use of archaic phrases. "It's the Staff Training Department," she confided, handing him the receiver. "They want to talk to you about your Hungarian lessons."

A few weeks later Lazenby had been instructed to

attend his security clearance interview, which he quite enjoyed . . .

"Well, well, good afternoon, Lazenby. Heard the news? Some nutter's taken a pot shot at Reagan."

"Is he dead?"

"How could they tell?" The man behind the desk laughed uproariously at his own sally.

"Dorothy Parker said something like that, about Hoover," Lazenby pointed out unsmilingly.

"Ah, was that who it was? Well anyway, long time no see, old boy."

Lazenby blinked. The man in the interview room to which he had been escorted by a chirpy black youth with a ripe Brixton accent was, he thought, a complete stranger to him. "Do I know you?" he enquired politely.

"Lot of water's flowed under the bridge since we last met, I suppose. Understandable you might not recognise your old schoolmate."

Given this clue and after peering intently at his interrogator, Lazenby discerned the lineaments of youth still dimly visible behind the raddled, flabby features of the man opposite. "Good lord, you're Armstrong!" he cried, and was immediately hushed.

"Not so loud, for heavens sake! You're not supposed to know my name." Armstrong glanced briefly down through half-moon glasses at the single sheet of paper before him. "Well, Lazenby, the years sit lightly on you by the look of you. Keep yourself in trim, I'd say."

Lazenby charitably suppressed the retort that rose to his lips, namely that the years had clearly knocked the living daylights out of the once god-like Mark Armstrong. Armstrong had lorded it as a prefect and captain of cricket at the minor public school they had both attended; while Lazenby, one year his junior, had been contentedly active in the debating and dramatic societies.

"Good lord," he rather feebly repeated instead. "Fancy meeting you here."

Armstrong looked about him at the drab, sparsely furnished cell in the nondescript office building a stone's throw from Parliament Square. "Bit off-putting, I imagine? This interview room? My own office, I hasten to add, is somewhat less spartan. Ah well, to our muttons. My job is to put some flesh, as it were, on the bones of your cv." He chuckled unconvincingly. "Make sure you're as sound a fellow as everybody says you are. All right with you?"

Lazenby shrugged. "Fire away."

"Right. Well, since we last met, you've knocked about a bit, I see. A good second in history from Reading, then a spot of schoolmastering while you did your MA, then the British Council. Well, I suppose you couldn't very well try for the Office with that sort of record." He flicked a fleck of dandruff from his lapel and preened himself. "I went up to Oxford myself, as you probably remember."

Nettled, Lazenby rose to the bait. "Didn't even think about the diplomatic service. Couldn't see myself parroting the government line while composing reports full of gossip picked up at cocktail parties."

Armstrong wagged a roguish finger, but sounded rather put out. "Naughty, naughty. All being well, you're about to become a diplomat yourself."

"True, but a specialist in cultural affairs."

"Well, we'll let that pass for the moment. I might as well tell you that I know about that curious business you seem to have been mixed up in while you were in India. Not to mention the trouble you caused for a lot of people when you were in Japan. Still, the British Council seems to have forgiven you so I suppose we must. I see you're recently divorced. Messy, I expect?"

"Not particularly."

"I'm glad to hear it, but somewhat surprised. I gather the former Mrs Lazenby had a, how shall I put it, somewhat roving eye. But she's not being PV'd, is she? You are." He smiled without involving his eyes. "Fond of a drink, are you, old boy?"

Lazenby tried and failed to maintain a calm manner. Staring pointedly at the broken veins in Armstrong's nose, he uttered a brief snort. "Not in the sense you're implying. Are you, *old boy*?"

A long, taut silence ensued before Armstrong spoke again, in an unexpectedly conciliatory way. "Dash it all, Lazenby, I'm the one asking the questions, so let's get on, shall we? No children, I see. What about gambling debts?"

Lazenby smiled for the first time. "You make it sound as though that's the only alternative to children. No, I've never done more in that line than join in the office Derby sweepstake."

"Good. Might make you vulnerable, you see. If you ran up debts and then some johnny came along dangling large sums of money in front of you."

"In return for a sight of the plans of the Royal Navy's dispositions at Gibraltar, you mean? Or the proofs of the British Council's next annual report?"

Armstrong sighed theatrically. "You're not doing yourself any good, you know, by adopting this attitude. This is a serious business, and for your own sake you should resist the temptation to give frivolous answers. Now there's one important area I haven't yet touched on: sex. I know the social climate's not what it was, but all the same . . . So far as anybody knows, you've kept your nose clean. By which I mean you haven't indulged in unorthodox sexual practices that might make you a subject for blackmail. Right?"

Nodding owlishly, Lazenby solemnly agreed, then spoiled the effect by adding "But that's probably because nobody's ever asked me, Armstrong. You doing anything this evening?"

* * *

Meantime, in Hungary they were going through their own routine preparations for the arrival of a new member of the diplomatic corps.

"All right, we'll give our approval," said the head of the protocol department at the Hungarian Ministry of Foreign Affairs. He initialled and stamped the document in front of him and handed it back to the desk officer for the United Kingdom. "The AVH will no doubt want to open a dossier on him. And of course you'll advise your opposite number in the Institute of Cultural Relations. He'll be working with him on a day-to-day basis, after all. Who is it these days?"

"Fellow called Szekacs. Viktor Szekacs."

"What's he like?"

The desk officer shrugged. "All right, I suppose. Very dedicated."

Following his interview with Armstrong, Lazenby was summoned again to the Personnel Department and told, somewhat to his surprise, that neither the Foreign Office Security Department nor the Hungarian government had raised any objections to his proceeding to Budapest and taking up the post of First Secretary and Cultural Attaché at the British Embassy there, and that he would receive formal written notice of his posting and promotion in a day or so. In the meantime he was to discuss direct with the director of the East Europe Department the details of his briefing programme and press on with his Hungarian lessons.

Lazenby thought about letting Susan know what he was upto, but then shrugged. Better to leave her in peace to concentrate on her new life with Giles.

Chapter One

March 1982

Lazenby stood in the transit lounge at Ferìgehy airport and watched the British Airways plane from London taxi slowly off the runway, approach the terminal building and come to a standstill.

In the six months he had been at the post he had learned quite a lot about what being a diplomat on the wrong side of the Iron Curtain entailed. There were privileges it was all too easy to get used to: duty-free booze, smokes and petrol, access to well-stocked hard currency stores and the special butcher's shop at which fillet and sirloin steaks were available to diplomats and senior Hungarian officials only.

Lazenby's most important and useful possession was the Ministry of Foreign Affairs identity card, bearing a photograph which he thought made him look like a wanted criminal, and describing him in Hungarian as an *Elso Titkar*, or First Secretary, and therefore a personage of some consequence in the distinctly minor league western diplomatic community of Budapest.

The Soviet Embassy was littered with Ministers and Counsellors, but there were no such grandees to aid and comfort the British Ambassador. His second in command was the Head of Chancery, a smooth Old Etonian who had in a previous post acquired the nickname Loo Brush when a colleague pointed out that he could and sometimes did go right round the bend. The sobriquet had preceded him to Budapest, in a private, gossipy letter sent from London by one in the know to a friend, and was used by all Embassy staff behind his back. As the Ambassador's deputy Loo Brush acted as Chargé d'Affaires in the great man's absences from Hungary, but even he was in rank also a First Secretary (though a *proper* one, as he had lost no time in pointing out to Lazenby when welcoming him aboard).

Lazenby had moved into the house provided for successive British Cultural Attachés since the late forties, and gave thanks frequently to the unknown but obviously civilised Hungarian civil servant responsible for housing foreign diplomats decades earlier, who must have decided that it was appropriate for such use. It was a splendid, rambling old place, full of huge pieces of Biedermeyer-style furniture in one of the most select residential streets on Castle Hill on the Buda side of the Danube. Lazenby was well aware that these were without question the grandest quarters he would ever occupy in his life.

That wasn't all, however. His new dark green left-hand drive Rover car sported special blue number plates. These meant that he could park in places which were off limits to the *hoi polloi*, the only snag being that they also proclaimed his identity to every police officer or government spy he passed.

In addition to adjusting to life in East Europe, Lazenby had been obliged to learn the exotic domestic rituals that consumed much of the time and energy of his colleagues in the Embassy, and to realise with mingled amusement and scorn that their priorities were very different from those he had developed in the less inhibited culture of his own organisation. There were practical consequences, too, since his anomalous position as a British Council cuckoo in a Foreign Office nest did not exempt him from routine housekeeping chores. As one of only seven Embassy staff members with full diplomatic status, Lazenby was required to share the duties undertaken by all the others with the sole exception of the Ambassador himself. One of the more time-consuming jobs came round every month or so and was the reason for Lazenby's presence at the airport on that bright afternoon in early spring. It was his turn to do the weekly Bag Run.

A couple of dozen passengers were disembarking from the plane, which was due to continue on to Bucharest after refuelling, but it was easy for Lazenby to spot the Queen's Messenger. In the first place he was one of just two people making their way to the transit lounge rather than joining the queue for immigration and customs, and secondly he was carrying an official-looking briefcase chained to his wrist, and two white canvas sacks. His companion, a man in BA uniform, was lugging two much bulkier sacks of the same type.

Lazenby stepped forward and introduced himself. "Major Hayward? Good afternoon. I'm Ben Lazenby."

The QM was every inch the retired military man, dapper in a blazer, Viyella shirt, regimental tie and cavalry twill trousers with a miraculous crease. His hair was in disciplined retreat from his brow, and his eyes were narrowed keenly. "How d'ye do. First time we've met, I believe. Mind showing me your card?"

"No, of course not." Lazenby hurriedly produced the vital identity card and held it out for Hayward to scrutinise since the QM's hands were occupied with his briefcase and the bags. While doing this Lazenby turned his head slightly and smiled sheepishly at the British Airways man, who seemed to be regarding him with even greater suspicion.

"Splendid," Hayward said, looking into Lazenby's face and then briefly down again at the photograph in his pass. "You can leave those here, if you will, old man," he added to his cohort, who duly relinquished his hold on the two big sacks and made off without having uttered a word.

Satisfied about Lazenby's *bona fides*, Hayward was now all affability. "Lazenby, eh? I knew a Tubby Lazenby once, a Gunner. No relation, I s'pose? No? Oh well, it was a long shot really. There's a luggage trolley over there. Be a good chap and fetch it, would you? You're going to need it."

Lazenby wheeled the trolley to the two big sacks and loaded them on to it, and the Major added one of his small ones to the pile. "Right. Trouble you to sign for all three, the two unclassified ones on *this* sheet and the confidential one on *this*". As he spoke, with that oddly strangulated but clipped intonation so characteristic of regular British Army officers that they must teach it at Sandhurst, Hayward whipped the necessary papers out of his briefcase with his unfettered hand, and Lazenby signed the receipts.

"Taking the other one on to Bucharest, are you?" he enquired politely. The QM nodded. "That's right. Then overnight there and straight back to Blighty tomorrow. Know Bucharest at all, Lazenby?"

"Not yet, but I'll be going there next month. What's it like?"

"Pleasant little Embassy, French style building. But grim, old boy, grim. You're far better off here, believe me. Well, I must be off back to the plane." He turned away, then at once wheeled round again. "Dear me, nearly forgot." He opened his briefcase again and took out a package wrapped in newspaper inside a clear plastic bag. "Give this to Alan for me, will you? And tell him I hope he can put me up next month when I'm on this run again. I'll be stopping over on my way back." He leaned towards Lazenby and lowered his voice conspiratorially. "Pair of kippers. Not too niffy I hope. Well, bung ho."

As he watched the QM emerge again from the terminal

and step out briskly towards the plane that would bear him and his confidential burden to Romania, Lazenby sniffed dubiously at the package, which was indeed giving off a slight kipperish aroma. He wondered if the good man had another pair with him to present to his prospective host and hostess in Bucharest, or whether they were to receive a pound of Wall's sausages instead.

The life of a Queen's Messenger was a rum sort of do, he reflected as he began to trundle his trolley towards the exit. He glanced down at the three bags, fastened tightly and secured with seals of lead, and wondered if there really were any interesting secret papers in the confidential one, and whether flying retired officers first class all over the world represented money well spent. Well, at least it meant a rare breakfast treat for one lucky devil, he decided as the little parcel of kippers in the plastic bag tumbled off its perch and he bent to pick it up and place it more securely on top of the diplomatic bags, and made his way past a casually saluting customs officer and through to the outer concourse. There his escort, a burly British security officer, was waiting for him and together they saw the bags safely stowed in the boot of the Embassy car parked outside.

Lazenby kept the kippers on the seat beside him all the way back to the Embassy, where he handed them over to Alan with a slight sense of grievance. It had been a long time since he'd eaten a kipper himself, and he was envious.

"All right, that's quite enough about Argentinian scrap metal dealers. A lot of fuss about nothing, in my view. Now, what's happening on the culture front? I see *Chariots of Fire* won an Oscar, whatever that may be. I suppose that's a good thing. Well, has the British Council any goodies in store for us, Ben? Anything in the morris dancing line, say? I wonder what the proper collective noun for morris dancers is, a tinkle, perhaps?" The Ambassador leaned back in his leather armchair and scrutinised his nails, then teased with one of them at a cuticle on the other hand. He was in his early fifties, looking forward to moving up to a Grade 2 post next time and the KCMG that would go with it.

The other diplomats gathered for "morning prayers" in the Ambassador's room tittered dutifully at the tired old jibe and Lazenby was tempted to take umbrage, but resisted. He could cross his eyes and resemble the silent film comedian Ben Turpin at will, however, and he did so now, just in time to meet the Ambassador's level gaze as he suddenly raised his head from his DIY manicure.

"Not in the foreseeable future, Ambassador. But I'm working on it," he said, hastily readjusting his expression. "The Hungarian side have approved our nomination of Emma Jarvis under the Cultural Agreement to fill the vacancy for a British lecturer at Debrecen University. She's due to arrive the day after tomorrow, but she'll be met at the airport and taken care of by people from the KKI. Sorry, the Cultural Affairs Institute. I'll go along to greet her but I shouldn't think they'll allow me to do more than shake her hand. I thought I'd put in a formal request to visit her in Debrecen next month when she's had time to find her feet. I'll be passing that way en route to Bucharest."

"Bucharest? What the dickens are you going there for?"

Lazenby permitted himself a slightly ostentatious sigh. "To escort the lorries bringing about a million pounds' worth of paintings from there to here. For the exhibition of British landscape art to be displayed at the National Fine Art Gallery for a month. The paintings are being air-freighted out from London to Bucharest, and when the whole thing's over they'll go back by air from here. But the bit in between has to be done by road, accompanied by a responsible officer. As my Fine Arts Department colleague from London explained to you in this very room a couple of weeks ago. Sir."

"Ah, yes. No need to get huffy, Ben, I do dimly recall the conversation. Fellow with a bow tie, wasn't it. What's this Emma girl like, then? Should I give her lunch, or dinner?"

"Not yet, Ambassador. As I've explained, the Hungarians will be very proprietorial about her at first. They're paying her, after all. I was on her final selection board in London and she seems very pleasant."

"Not one of these dreadful feminist harpies, then. Good."

Out of the corner of his eye Lazenby saw Joanna Crockett biting her lip in impotent rage. She was twenty-seven, a Third Secretary on the commercial side and the only woman present. Joanna was in her first substantive overseas post, and was learning painfully that one of the few respects in which ambassadors really can be said to be plenipotentiary nowadays is in making or breaking the careers of fledgling diplomats. So it paid to pretend to ignore slights.

Lazenby was not inhibited by such considerations, and not prone to excessive reverence anyway. His own promotion prospects were a matter for the British Council's senior staff, who rather prided themselves on listening to heavy hints from the head of the Foreign Office's own Cultural Department and then doing the reverse of what he appeared to be suggesting. He was moved to take up the cudgels on Joanna's behalf. "Emma Jarvis is an intelligent, highly qualified person with a Ph.D. Like Joanna here. And I expect she's just as sensitive to casual male chauvinism."

For a long moment he'd thought he'd overdone it. The silence that followed was eloquent. A dusky rose colour suffused Joanna Crockett's neck, while Loo Brush's glasses flashed warningly. The Military Attaché affected a sudden interest in his clip-board, and the Second Secretary (Political) smiled secretively. Then, to Lazenby's relief, the Ambassador grinned with considerable charm. "Point taken, dear boy," he said. "*Mea culpa.* Well, present my compliments to the learned Doctor Jarvis when you see her, and tell her that I look forward to making her acquaintance. When did you say you're off to Bucharest?"

"The seventeenth of next month, sir. I'll be away just under a week in all. My KKI minder insists on going with me as far as the border."

"Is that the consumptive-looking young man you call Dracula?"

"The same, sir."

"I don't envy you, Ben. Well, have fun, and don't lose the paintings, there's a good chap."

Chapter Two

Standing at one of the windows of his stately first-floor living room, Lazenby gazed down at the bloated black Chaika saloon car drawing up outside. It came to a halt behind his Rover, in which he had earlier placed a suitcase containing a formal suit and a few other belongings plus some hard-to-obtain supplies for Emma Jarvis. Rozsika, the daily cook-general supplied by the state domestic agency, was bustling about the nether regions of the house and would answer the doorbell if it rang, but Lazenby knew from past experience that Dracula would refuse any invitation to cross his decadent capitalist threshhold. It had of course occurred to him that this reluctance to enter the house might have been due to the contrast its splendour must have made with his own domestic arrangements. Yet as a Party member Viktor Szekacs was almost certainly housed in a comfortable apartment and had access to valuable perks.

Lazenby sighed. No, it was simply that Szekacs was so ideologically blinkered as to be incapable of spontaneity in human relationships. No doubt that was why, as Lazenby had made it his business to find out, he was unmarried. In any event, he was very hard to like.

Lazenby checked that he had his passport and wallet in the pocket of his sports jacket, and other necessary papers in his briefcase with the file of correspondence about the exhibition. Then he made his way downstairs. Rozsika, a beefy lady in her late forties, was vigorously dusting the vast hatstand in the stone-flagged hall, and he bade her a cheery farewell before unlocking and opening his front door, a massive, creaking affair which wouldn't have disgraced a small cathedral.

He hadn't bothered to mention to Rozsika that he was going to be away for a few days: she knew virtually everything a Hungarian could know about his official business and a great deal about his personal affairs anyway, and would have been briefed about the trip to Romania by the security officer she reported to when handing in the contents of his waste-paper basket.

As Lazenby emerged into the spring sunshine and Rozsika closed the door behind him, Viktor Szekacs stepped out of the front passenger seat of the Russian car, which resembled the ill-fated Ford Edsel of the fifties, leaving the door open. "Good morning, Mr Lazenby. The weather is fine," he said disapprovingly, as though he would have preferred it to be otherwise.

Though under thirty, Szekacs had the gravity of manner of an elderly man of respectable habits. He also dressed like one. It was his unusual thinness and the pallor of his complexion that had first prompted Lazenby to bestow the nickname "Dracula" on him, and the longer their acquaintance continued the more apt it seemed. Viktor spoke good if slightly stilted English, as befitted the KKI's desk officer for all matters arising from the Anglo-Hungarian Cultural Agreement, and was invariably correct in his dealings with Lazenby, whose tendency to levity clearly disconcerted him.

"Morning, Viktor. Yes, it is a nice day considering it's Monday. You riding in that tank, or are you going to keep me company in my car?"

"Before I answer your question, allow me to introduce Comrade Nagy, one of the Cultural Institute's chauffeurs." Comrade Nagy was a stocky man of about forty who remained at the wheel of his leviathan and merely nodded his head curtly when Lazenby leant into the open passenger door and greeted him affably. He had learned basic Hungarian before leaving London, and had worked on it to some effect since arriving in Budapest.

"Your Hungarian is coming along well, Mr Lazenby," Dracula said, nodding in a frostily indulgent way.

"I do wish you'd call me Ben," Lazenby said, while realising that if he'd been quicker witted he could have asked Nagy in colloquial Hungarian how he was doing. This would have sounded like *Hodge vodge, Nodge?*", which would have been pleasingly euphonious.

"That would not be proper, though I am gratified that you address me by my own given name. Our journey today will take us some four hours. I propose that I should remain in this vehicle with Comrade Nagy and that we should lead you to the main road to Debrecen, our route being by way of Szolnok. Then, after a while, I shall accept your invitation and be your passenger. Though of course we shall continue to be led by Comrade Nagy."

Lazenby was already tolerably well acquainted with the road to Debrecen, but knew that there was no point in debating the issue, for this expedition had been planned in detail as soon as Lazenby put in his formal request to visit Debrecen University on his way to Romania. They were due to arrive by the middle of the afternoon at the Golden Ox, the best hotel in town, where they would all pass the night. He, escorted by Szekacs, was to call on the head of the English Department the following morning before proceeding to the nearby border with Romania, where Szekacs would turn back and return to Budapest. As a tremendous concession Dracula had agreed that Lazenby might invite Emma Jarvis out to dine privately with him at a restaurant in the evening, and over the telephone she had accepted with alacrity.

It wasn't until they were well clear of the city and the traffic had thinned out so much that they had the road largely to themselves that it dawned on Lazenby that Comrade Nagy's driving technique was distinctly idiosyncratic. Several times the Chaika accelerated steadily until it reached breakneck speed, only to slow down again gradually to a virtual crawl. Unable to account in any other way for their swooping progress, he concluded that Comrade Nagy was amusing himself by putting his foot down until the Chaika could go no faster, then ignoring the accelerator pedal altogether until the car was about to stall before repeating the process.

They had covered some fifteen miles in this fashion when the car in front stopped altogether near a minor side road, and Lazenby pulled the Rover in behind it. Szekacs emerged and had barely closed the door behind him when the big black car sped off with a screech of tyres and turned down the side road, leaving Dracula looking slightly forlorn and, Lazenby thought as he leaned over to open his own passenger door, embarrassed.

"Welcome aboard, Viktor. Where's Comrade Nagy off to, then?"

"Um, he has some business in a nearby village. He will catch us up later."

Lazenby glanced down the side road as the Rover passed by the junction. The featureless plain known as the *puszta* lay some way ahead of them, but the countryside they were passing through was flat and sparsely populated, and all he could see in what must have been at least two miles was a small church and the adjoining priest's house, both painted in the usual dull Habsburg yellow. "Cultural Institute business? There's only a church down there," he said. Obviously ill at ease, Dracula was making quite a business of settling himself in the passenger seat.

"Well, not exactly. In point of fact it is personal business. The um, priest is his brother-in-law."

"Dear me. That must be awkward for Comrade Nagy. He's a Party member like you, I presume?"

"Party membership is not required of all Cultural Institute staff, but in any case there is no reason to suppose that my colleague shares the superstitious beliefs of his wife's brother."

Lazenby decided that a little gentle teasing was in order. "Still, it's a bit unusual to take off in the office car on personal business in the middle of an official journey, I should have thought. On a working day."

"All Hungarian workers are conscious at all times of their responsibility to be diligent in the performance of their duties. As I have just explained, Comrade Nagy will catch us up long before we reach Debrecen."

Dracula relapsed into an offended silence and Lazenby decided to postpone comment on the absent driver's alternately madcap and funereal driving style. It wasn't until nearly two hours later, when they were well past Szolnok and had stopped at a roadside inn for refreshment that Comrade Nagy did indeed put in a brief appearance. Lazenby and Szekacs were sitting at a table in the sunshine outside, drinking coffee and eating crusty bread rolls with hot sausages and mustard at the time. The Chaika approached at great speed and Szekacs leapt to his feet, waving furiously; but they were vouchsafed merely a fleeting glimpse of Nagy in silhouette through the windows as he swerved, missing the Rover by inches, and hurtled by in a cloud of dust.

"He must have another bit of private business to attend to," Lazenby suggested slyly, but there was no reply.

Soon after three in the afternoon, he and Szekacs approached the ornate reception desk of the Golden Ox. Szekacs did the talking, since the bookings had been made through his office. Meantime Lazenby stood by his suitcase looking round appreciatively at the stodgily comfortable lounge. He liked the look of the polished dark wood and heavy, overstuffed armchairs, each with a lace antimacassar in place. He couldn't overhear the conversation at the desk, because there was an extraordinary racket emanating from the inner regions, involving lively gipsy music and male and female voices raised bonhomously in what sounded, judging from the raucous laughter and merry screams, like a bucolic orgy.

After a while Szekacs came over to him, looking smug. "You are no doubt accustomed to great luxury, so a suite has been reserved for your exclusive use, Mr Lazenby. I shall share a much humbler room with Comrade Nagy."

"Splendid," Lazenby bellowed over the din. He liked the sound of a suite. He was paying for his own accommodation but the bill could be charged to his travel and subsistence allocation. "Where's Nagy, by the way? I saw the Chaika outside."

"I was informed that in a very democratic manner he accepted an invitation to join the wedding party you can no doubt hear."

"Crikey. That man seems to live purely for pleasure. And the workers of Debrecen sound as if they know how to enjoy themselves during office hours, too."

"May I remind you that reasonable recreation, especially in connection with a wedding celebration, has a proper place in a socialist society? The party will I am sure be over shortly." Szekacs was clearly miffed, and Lazenby decided that enough was enough.

"Right, Viktor. When shall we meet again?"

"Our appointment at the University is at ten in the morning. May I suggest that you take your breakfast at a time convenient for you and that we meet at the reception desk here at, say, nine-fifteen? Until then, please enjoy some sight-seeing in the city and your evening in the company of Miss Jarvis."

"Thanks, I will. I'll go and freshen up, then, and see you in the morning. Sleep well."

* * *

Lazenby's suite was in an annexe and consisted of two connecting rooms and a bathroom. One contained a massive old-fashioned bed and a capacious wardrobe, the other a sofa and an ornate desk; and the elderly and badly stained bath stood in splendid isolation on clawed feet alongside a lavatory with a wooden seat surrounded by colourful art deco tiles that would, it occurred to Lazenby, fetch absurdly high prices in Camden Passage. It was opulently comfortable and blessedly quiet, and rather than exploring the town he took a nap before bathing and sprucing himself up to meet Emma Jarvis, who had said she would look for him in the lobby at about seven.

In the peace of his suite he had almost forgotten the afternoon wedding party, and was surprised when he made his way back to the main building to keep their rendezvous to realise that it was not only still going strong, but, on the evidence of the noise level in the lobby, had shifted into an even higher gear.

It proved to be a useful ice-breaker, for when Dr Jarvis came in through the front entrance she stopped short and an expression of incredulity crossed her features as the whoops, yelling and blast of music assailed her. Lazenby moved over to her with a smile and an outstretched hand, and pitched his voice at an encouraging shout.

"I was going to suggest a drink in the bar, but if we're going to have any sort of conversation it might be better to go straight to the restaurant."

She nodded fervently, and waited until they were outside before attempting to reply. Then she exhaled with relief. "That's better. I hope they aren't going to make a night of it, for your sake. Anyway, nice to see you, Mr Lazenby."

"And very good to see you again, Dr Jarvis."

He beamed at her appreciatively. When he had seen her at the airport a few weeks earlier she had been tired after her journey and understandably nervous, and the change in her appearance was striking. She was wearing a light woollen coat over a blue silk blouse and a skirt that emphasised the slenderness of her waist and the trimness of her legs and ankles; her hazel eyes were calm and the expression on her face amused and composed. Emma Jarvis had clearly made an effort to look good, and knew that she had succeeded.

"You said on the phone that one of your English Department colleagues had recommended a good place to eat."

"Mm. I've already been there twice. I hope you're an enthusiastic carnivore."

"Is there anything else to be in Hungary? Should we take a taxi? I have my car here but I'm looking forward to a drink, so I don't want to drive."

"Taxi? Good heavens, no. It's only a couple of hundred yards away."

Lazenby had been mentally prepared for young Dr Jarvis to be wary with him, even prickly: after all, he did represent officialdom. She seemed entirely at ease, however, and by the time they had arrived at the folksy Nimrod Restaurant and been shown to a polished wooden table with a bright red cloth she had accepted his invitation to call him Ben and stated unnecessarily that she was Emma. Lazenby decided that he was going to enjoy his evening.

They each had a glass of dry Tokay as an aperitif, and then shared a huge plate of mixed sliced sausage, washed down with a bottle of Badacsonyi Keknyelu. "Treating you reasonably well, then, it seems," Lazenby said. While enthusiastically tucking into her food, Emma Jarvis had given him a beautifully lucid account of her experiences since her arrival.

"No real complaints", she said briskly. "They've provided me with a perfectly adequate small flat, and the teaching load isn't heavy. In any case, I like the students and most of the staff. Professor Horvath in particular. She's an old duck. You'll meet her tomorrow. The speciality here's the Robber's Platter, by the way. It's a kind of mixed grill. Better in mid-winter, I'm told, but . . ."

"But we could do worse than have it."

"Right. I'm sure I've already put on pounds since I arrived, but I don't care." She pulled a face. "I must say I do miss citrus fruit and proper vegetables, though."

"Ah, the eternal gherkins." Further speech was precluded for a while by the arrival at their table of a moustachioed violinist in colourful gipsy attire, who beamed soulfully at Emma, leaned over her and tried to see down the front of her blouse while he rendered a saccharine melody to the accompaniment of tinkling arpeggios supplied by a cimbalom player at the back of the room.

Producing and handing over the fifty-forint note which he had been advised was the customary bribe to persuade the musician to go to another table, Lazenby made a mental note to bring Emma back a great bag of oranges the next time he drove to Vienna. He could go there whenever he liked: but she had none of the privileges he enjoyed and could look forward to being granted just one exit/re-entry visa a year during her three-year stint.

Left to themselves again, they dealt with their Robber's Platter with gusto, and polished off a bottle of Bull's Blood with it; then finished with *Somloi Galuska*, a sort of Hungarian trifle, which tasted much better than the English translation on the menu – "Noodles of the Somlo Region" – suggested it should. With coffee they each had a glass of apricot brandy, and were both pleasantly tipsy by the time Lazenby escorted her back to the dreary apartment block in which she lived.

Just in time he remembered to hand over the plastic bag he had brought for her. It contained two boxes of Kleenex, a jar of Nescafé, a tin of Band-aids and a plastic bottle each of Stergene and Squezy washing-up liquid from the Embassy staff shop. Joanna Crockett had recommended these items as more than acceptable gifts for a young British lady living on her own in the Hungarian provinces, and contributed a rectangular package wrapped in brown paper and a letter from herself. Lazenby thought he could guess what was in the package and thought Emma would be grateful for this token of sisterly thoughtfulness; but was astounded when she positively crooned over the bottle of Squezy, tears of gratitude brimming in her eyes.

"Oh, you *lovely* man," she sighed at last, gazing up at him. Lazenby smiled, sharply conscious of her scent and aware that sexual chemistry was at its magical work. For him, certainly, and – or perhaps it was just the wine in her case – maybe for Emma too. He cleared his throat.

"Oh, its nothing. My pleasure. Well, er, goodnight again. See you in the morning," he said, sternly resisting a strong temptation to kiss her slightly open mouth, and turned away.

"Goodnight," Emma said in a small voice. "I'd like to ask you in for a cup of coffee or something, but people . . ." He turned to face her again, took her warm hand in his and raised it to his lips in the Hungarian manner.

"Yes, I quite understand. See you tomorrow."

It was only a few minutes' walk back to the Golden Ox, where he arrived just before eleven. The sounds of the wedding party could still be heard as he collected his key, and he shook his head slowly as he made his way to his suite, wondering if Comrade Nagy was persevering with his exercise in democratic bonhomie.

Lazenby cleaned his teeth and went to bed in high, if muzzy, good humour. The delightful Emma was highly unlikely to constitute a welfare problem in the future; and their meal, copious drink and all, had cost him less than twenty pounds. He slept very well that night, and was blessed with an enjoyably improper dream.

Chapter Three

Having settled his modest bill, Lazenby had spent some time watching the comings and goings in the hotel lobby when Viktor Szekacs put in a belated appearance, looking like a Dracula thwarted in the previous night's search for a comely white neck to sink his fangs into, and more than usually eager to pass the daylight hours in a comfy coffin.

The wretched man shuffled to the cashier's part of the desk, wincing visibly when a hearty young woman behind it banged an old-fashioned bell to summon a porter. He winced again when Lazenby went over to him and offered a cheery greeting. "Morning, Viktor! Sleep well?"

Szekacs turned his head with care and focused blearily on him. "No, Mr Lazenby, I admit that I did not sleep well," he croaked. "Our room was directly above the private banqueting room, and the wedding party continued noisily into the small hours. Then Comrade Nagy banged on the door until I got up to let him in. That was at about three-thirty, and he wanted to talk." The poor fellow gazed at him with such haggard pathos in his face that Lazenby couldn't bring himself to torment him any more.

"Oh, rotten luck, Viktor."

"Mr Lazenby. I must ask if we may go to the University in your car."

"Of course. Nagy has a hangover, I take it?"

Szekacs managed a ghost of a smile for about a quarter

of a second. "Yes. What I believe is known in your English idiom as a father and mother of hangovers. Which I am obliged to say I think he deserves. He will bring the car to the border later today and take me back to Budapest after you have crossed into Romania."

Cheered by this perceptible chink in the solidarity Dracula had hitherto doggedly expressed in regard to his wayward colleague, Lazenby maintained a sympathetic silence until their bags were stowed away in the boot of his car and they were on the way to the campus. His passenger coughed delicately and seemed to be on the verge of speech several times before finally managing to produce actual words.

"You had a pleasant meal with Miss Jarvis, I hope?"

"Yes indeed. And I'm glad to report that she seems to be settling in very well. She says Professor Horvath has been particularly kind. Describes her as an old duck, in fact."

"An old . . . duck?"

"It's a great compliment, Viktor. A term of considerable affection."

Professor Judit Horvath was indeed an an old duck. A buxom, silver-haired lady who looked as if she was in her sixties but was very possibly much younger, she welcomed her visitors to her room with great warmth, directing a smile of particular sweetness at Lazenby. When he took her proffered hand and bent over it, murmuring *"Kezed csokolom"* as he did so, she gazed at him so meltingly that she seemed to be on the point of swooning.

"Why, Mr Lazenby, your Hungarian is so fluent, and beautifully pronounced!" Professor Horvath spoke English in a charmingly ladylike way, and since all Lazenby had said was "I kiss your hand" he concluded that she must be a fervent Anglophile.

"You shouldn't flatter me, Professor Horvath. Mr

Szekacs here knows very well that I'm just a beginner. You've just heard about ten per cent of my entire Hungarian vocabulary. It's very good of you to receive me this morning. I spoke to Emma Jarvis yesterday evening and she told me how very kind you've been to her since she arrived."

Dr Horvath clasped her hands together in apparent ecstasy, ignoring Szekacs who sank uninvited into a chair and sat there looking for all the world like a suffering poet rather than a dedicated official and Party member. "*Dear* Mr Lazenby, it is a joy to hear the Queen's English again, from you and of course from Emma. A dear child, who tells me that she was born in Dorset, which I have been privileged to visit. To think that we have a native of the Hardy country here in Debrecen!"

"I'm afraid I come from London, which isn't anything to boast about."

"Come, come, Mr Lazenby! I must venture to chide you. Think of Charles Dickens! And remember the words of that eminent son of Lichfield, Samuel Johnson. 'The man who is tired of London' – "

"– 'is tired of life.'" Lazenby smiled, and they might have gone on exchanging sugary pleasantries indefinitely, had not Szekacs muttered something in rapid Hungarian which made Dr Horvath look rather crestfallen. Casting a sad little glance at Lazenby she went to the door and murmured to somebody in the corridor outside. A moment later Emma Jarvis walked into the room, followed by another young woman who was wearing a faded blue smock and bearing a tray on which were four cups of coffee. Dr Horvath took the tray from her and set it down on her desk, whereupon the young woman looked terrified and scuttled out without having spoken.

Lazenby was still standing, and noted with interest that Szekacs dragged himself to his feet and bent over Emma's hand, though more perfunctorily than Lazenby had done with their hostess. "We met at the airport a few weeks ago. I am Viktor Szekacs. From the Institute for Cultural Relations. Good morning, Dr Jarvis."

"Morning, Mr Szekacs," Emma said. "Well, as you can see, I'm alive and well and at my place of employment." She glanced over at Lazenby and grinned before turning to face Szekacs again. "You look a bit under the weather yourself, though, if I may say so."

Szekacs wilted under the not very friendly scrutiny of three pairs of eyes. "I, ah, yes. I do have a slight headache, so perhaps I will excuse myself at this point and go out into the fresh air. Shall I meet you by your car in, say, half an hour, Mr Lazenby?"

Professor Horvath might have been getting on in years, but she bounded to the door like an eager puppy and had it open in a millisecond, inclining her head curtly as he slunk out. Closing the door behind him, she beamed with relief. "Now, why don't you both sit down and we can have a nice chat over this frightful, tepid coffee," she said cosily.

A pair of bedraggled but bright-eyed gipsy children waylaid Lazenby as he approached his car. Szekacs had been lurking some distance away and was walking towards them from the opposite direction.

"Hello, boss! Twenty forints, yes?"

Lazenby stared at the little girl, who couldn't have been more than nine or ten years old. "Twenty forints? What for?"

"For me. Agnes. And twenty for Sandor. Sandor my brother. We clean your car."

"Did you now?" Lazenby saw that something at least had been done to the Rover, in that the dust of the previous day's drive had been smeared unevenly over the paintwork. Impressed by her cheek and her command of English, he smiled and took out his wallet. He handed Agnes a ten forint note, and was taken

31

aback when she spat expertly on the ground at his feet.

"Stingy bastard," she said, but nevertheless stowed the note away swiftly into the pocket of the ragged cotton frock which looked as if it was all she had on her skinny little body. Meantime her brother, a year or so younger and dressed in a clearly home-made shirt and a voluminous pair of cut-down men's trousers, looked hopeful and held out his hand, but remained silent.

"Money for Sandor, too, stingy bastard," Agnes insisted, and Ben gave the little boy ten forints too, just as Szekacs arrived on the scene with a face like thunder, shouting something that Lazenby couldn't begin to translate but understood all too well.

"Calm down, Viktor," Lazenby protested mildly. "They're only little kids."

"They are thieves and *vermin*, and you are very wrong to encourage them, Mr Lazenby." Szekacs was almost choking with fury as the children scampered out of harm's way and Agnes, quickly imitated by the diminutive Sandor, began to dance about at a safe distance, pulling faces and yelling insults.

"Oh do get in, for heaven's sake." Having unlocked the front passenger door, Lazenby stood by it glaring until Szekacs gracelessly did as he was bidden. Then Lazenby followed suit and drove off, too annoyed with his minder even to tease him.

It was about fifty miles to the border, and Lazenby struck more or less due south and through the village of Derecske, turning left when he came to the junction with the highway to Oradea, the first town on the Romanian side of the border. A sullen silence persisted for about three quarters of an hour, thawing into awkward conversation which continued desultorily until they came to the first roadside sign indicating that they were approaching the frontier control post.

"Well, it looks as if this is where we part company," Lazenby said, making it clear by his tone that so far as he was concerned it wasn't a moment too soon. "Now listen, I'll be three nights in Romania, remember. You're sure that when I come back with the lorries – crossing from Arad, not here – there'll be no trouble on this side?"

Szekacs was stiffly formal. "Provided that you arrive at about the time we have agreed, you will be met by me and escorted without delay to the National Fine Art Gallery in Budapest." Then, unexpectedly revealing again the man behind the official mask, he sneered. "Of course, I can't predict what sort of chaos you'll experience at the hands of the stupid and inefficient Romanians."

Lazenby sighed, removed one hand from the wheel and wagged an admonitory finger at his passenger. "Viktor, Viktor, what's got into you today? First you blow your top at a couple of your junior compatriots, and now you're being rude about your fraternal socialist neighbours." Szekacs's thin lips were tightly compressed and it was obvious to Lazenby that no comment would be forthcoming. He sighed again extravagantly. "Never mind, I won't tell on you."

He slowed down as a Hungarian border guard stepped into the middle of the road and waved him in to the check-point, and as soon as the car had stopped Szekacs got out with what sounded distinctly like a snort. Lazenby watched him go into the little office building, and through its windows saw him in conversation with a uniformed official inside.

Then he rolled his window down and showed his passport and diplomatic identity card to a bored customs officer who merely glanced at the documents and at the diplomatic plates on the car, then waved him on; but Lazenby shook his head politely, got out of the car, unlocked the boot and waited beside it with folded arms. Skekacs emerged from his conference and came over.

"Well, good luck, Mr Lazenby. I must thank you for the transport." Lazenby let him heave his own bag out of the boot.

"You too, Viktor. I don't see any sign of Comrade Nagy and the Chaika, but no doubt he'll turn up when it suits him. Give him my regards. Cheerio. See you on Friday morning."

Lazenby resumed his seat and drove towards the barrier which was being raised to let him through, and without so much as a glance in the rear-view mirror bowled along the two-hundred-metre stretch of no man's land to the barrier on the Romanian side, expecting he knew not what.

His passage into Romania at a place called Bors couldn't have been less fraught. The official who examined his passport beamed happily when he saw the special visa Lazenby had been given by the Romanian Embassy in Budapest, saluted smartly and invited him into his office for a cup of even more evil-tasting coffee than the one he had barely managed to swallow in Professor Horvath's office.

It was half past two in the afternoon when Lazenby drove through Oradea and headed for Cluj, where he planned to spend the night so as to reach Bucharest well before nightfall the following day. For the next twenty minutes or so the countryside looked exactly like that on the Hungarian side of the border, but after that he saw wooded hills ahead and soon the road began to wind upwards, towards the range of mountains known as the Transylvanian Alps. He wound the window down and sniffed at the air, catching the resinous tang of pine, and drove more slowly, the more fully to appreciate it. At the same time he puzzled over Dracula's intemperate reaction to the gipsy children, and wondered what they would do with the meagre "earnings" Agnes had so pertly extorted from him. It was one of the minor pleasures of his life in Hungary to encounter free spirits. He thought it unlikely that individualism would manifest itself in what his colleagues had warned him was the dour and wretched society over which Great Leader Ceauşescu presided in Romania.

Just beyond a huddle of ramshackle houses and a small shop shown on his map as Borod, he slowed down even more in order to overtake safely an elderly woman in shapeless black clothes who was hobbling along, bent sideways by the weight of the bulky, crudely stitched shopping bag she was carrying. He was surprised when she turned and raised her free hand as peremptorily as any policeman on point duty. He was even more startled when, after he had obediently stopped and leaned out of the window to see what she wanted, the old lady tottered round to the passenger side and tried the door. Finding it locked, she rapped on the window and indicated impatiently that she required him to unlock the door, which Lazenby did, whereupon she opened it, heaved her bag inside and then herself scrambled into the passenger seat, straddling the bag awkwardly with her spindly black-clad legs.

"Huedin," she then quavered. At least, that is what it sounded like to Lazenby, who after giving her a wary glance consulted his map again, to discover that there was indeed a place of that name some twenty kilometres ahead.

He showed her the map, indicating the spot with his forefinger. "Huedin?"

His uninvited passenger ignored the map but nodded and settled herself in a manner that suggested she was wondering what Lazenby was waiting for, so in some confusion he let in the clutch and drove on. His map showed two other villages on the way to Huedin and he slowed to a crawl at each of them and looked over at the woman, who shook her head firmly each time and pointed ahead.

It seemed that she really did want to go all the way to

Huedin, and as he drove on Lazenby wondered if the old soul had actually set out to walk there, burdened as she was. The minor mystery was cleared up when they reached the place and he drew up at the crossroads that seemed to be its centre. The old woman began at once to struggle to open the door, so Lazenby he went round and helped her to extricate herself, then reached inside and hauled her bag from the floor, putting it on the ground beside her.

Lazenby expected at least a word of thanks, but instead she thrust a grubby banknote and some coins at him. He would have liked to know what the going fare was for a ride from Borod to Huedin, but smilingly declined the money with a gesture and what he hoped she interpreted as a courtly bow. Then he climbed back into the car and drove on, noticing in the rear view mirror that his unusual client was shrugging philosophically.

Though the old lady had left a distinct aroma as of old biscuits behind her in the Rover and was obviously not in the least eccentric by local standards, Lazenby had rather enjoyed his first meeting with an authentic private Romanian citizen, and left the window open to air the car until the increasing chill as the road wound ever higher prompted him to wind it up. He was in a good mood and singing one of the few hymns he remembered from his boyhood when he arrived in Cluj at dusk and pulled up outside what looked like a decent inn. Then he blinked in utter astonishment.

For two small figures emerged from the gloom and skipped towards the car, waving and whooping. Agnes and Sandor had somehow contrived to get there ahead of him.

Chapter Four

Lazenby's state of mind was such that he did not sleep well during the night he passed in Transylvania, and there were a number of reasons for this. First among these was the unnerving experience of being greeted on his arrival by the two young and penniless gipsy children, Hungarian to judge from their names, in another country and some two hundred miles from where he had left them earlier that day. Not only their materialisation in Cluj, but the fact that they seemed to have been expecting him there struck him as very odd and disturbing.

When he quizzed them outside the hotel, Agnes had been as perky and disrespectful as ever, while Sandor hung about kicking at a small stone and looking cheerful enough. Having persuaded Agnes not to go on addressing him as a stingy bastard, Lazenby had been able to elicit from her nothing but vague talk about uncles with lorries; and when he asked how they had contrived to cross a well-guarded frontier without papers Agnes merely spat again with scorn. "We don' care about *them*," she said witheringly. It was obvious that she dismissed papers, frontiers and border guards alike as being beneath contempt.

"Yes, but why have you come to Cluj?"
"Cluj? What you mean?"
"This place. It's called Cluj."
"Nah. This Koloszvar."

Lazenby knew that this part of Romania had formerly been Hungarian territory and that Cluj had indeed at one time been known as Koloszvar, but that had been long before Agnes and Sandor had been born. He had also encountered gipsy children before, having had his pocket skilfully picked within days of his arrival by an angelic little soul in Budapest's most fashionable shopping street. Nor was he too surprised by the racy colloquial English Agnes spoke. Street urchins who lived by their wits commonly picked up some useful words and phrases, and she was obviously a bright child.

He had learned since arriving in Budapest that gipsies in general and their children in particular were the despair of the communist bureaucracy. Viktor Szekacs's furious and hateful outburst outside Debrecen University was a depressing reminder of that. Many gipsies had neither papers nor any fixed abode, and roamed insouciantly all over the country, despised and discriminated against by most Magyars, but nevertheless surviving and giving the impression of jeering from the sidelines of a tightly controlled society. He must now get used to the idea that Central European gipsies took no more account of national boundaries than the Laplanders, and accept that it would take more than the combined efforts of Hungarian and Romanian frontier guards to frustrate the likes of Agnes and Sandor.

"Well, what are you going to do now you're here?"

"Watch car. See nobody take wipers, hub-caps, battery. You got *lei*?"

Lazenby had equipped himself with Romanian currency, but wasn't familiar with the rate of exchange. In any case, he was beginning to be seriously concerned about the children. "Never mind about *lei*. Where are you going to sleep tonight?"

Agnes shrugged her bony little shoulders. "In car?" she said hopefully. "If no *lei*, dollar okay."

"Dollar very okay, boss!" It was Sandor, whom Lazenby had previously heard using only Hungarian, when taunting

Dracula outside the drab University buildings. A little knot of bystanders had gathered and were taking in the scene with interest, and a man in shirt-sleeves emerged from the hotel entrance.

It was confusing and embarrassing, and Lazenby was tired. He turned to the man from the hotel. "Do you speak English?" he asked clearly and distinctly, and the man shook his head glumly. Lazenby had been told that French was spoken by educated Romanians; and though the man didn't look very sophisticated tried again.

"*Parlez vous français?*" Another dispiriting shake of the head. The man turned to the children and waved them away, shouting something in what to Lazenby's ears sounded uncommonly like Hungarian. The penny finally dropped, and it dawned on him that Agnes and Sandor had been right. Whatever the Romanian authorities called the place, it was still Koloszvar to the ethnic Hungarians who lived there; and the only reason he hadn't thought about the characteristics of the locals earlier was that the old woman who had regarded him as offering a freelance taxi service had uttered just one word during their half-hour acquaintance, and that a place name.

"*Beszel magyarul?*" he asked, and the man nodded still lugubriously but with the light of understanding in his eyes. Lazenby's Hungarian was up to asking if there was a room available for the night, and the man beckoned him towards the entrance, into which he turned and disappeared from view. Before following, Lazenby went over to the children.

"Listen," he said, delving into the back compartment of his wallet where he kept a reserve of sterling and American dollars for use in the hard currency shops of Budapest. He took out all the small denomination notes he had – three five-dollar and six one-dollar bills – and handed them to Agnes. "I shall probably stay here tonight. Get yourselves something to eat, and if you know anybody round here, go to them. Or go back where you came from. Understand? Now goodbye."

Both Agnes and Sandor obviously recognised the American money for what it was and their eyes glistened with delight. If they were as smart as they gave every indication of being, they could parlay twenty-one American dollars into more than enough food and Romanian currency to maintain themselves for a couple of days, and even perhaps have something left over for some clothing. "You bet! We come back soon, take care of your car!"

Lazenby watched them scamper off, and noticed a lump in his throat as he entered the hotel. Thirsty, probably, he told himself as he approached the little reception desk, behind which was a smiling young woman who greeted him in Hungarian and gave him a printed registration form. This was in Romanian and, to his relief, English. After he had filled it in and signed it, the woman doing duty as receptionist wanted to deprive him of his passport, but Lazenby firmly said "Diplomat" and hung on to it.

He managed to establish that there was a small space at the back of the building where he could park his car, and drove it round there. Removing his suitcase from the boot, he made sure that all four doors were locked. Then, after a moment of hesitation, he turned back and surreptitiously unlocked one of the rear doors again.

The plumbing in his room was inefficient, and the electrical wiring sagging in loops from the walls looked positively lethal, but at least there was enough tepid water for a shower, and the hotel had a restaurant attached which provided a boring but substantial meal and good red wine. He drank a whole bottle, became slightly fuddled, and was gratified when the young woman who had greeted him on his arrival approached his table and offered what he understood her to say was a glass of plum brandy with the compliments of the management. He accepted with tipsy courtliness. She brought what turned out to be a tumbler full and one for herself as well, and took a seat alongside him.

A warning bell sounded faintly in Lazenby's tired mind. Could this be an example of the notorious honey trap about which he'd been warned during his security briefing in London? Was he about to be ensnared, and photographed *in flagrante*? He discounted such prudent misgivings almost immediately. The important thing, the Foreign Office man had stressed, was to avoid putting yourself in a position where you could be blackmailed. He was a single man, after all. If the worst came to the worst he could always follow the example of the shameless Greek envoy, of honoured recent memory in diplomatic circles in Budapest. This stout fellow was visited in his office by a shady character who produced from his pocket a set of compromising photographs of the Greek and asked him what he proposed to do about them. Far from falling to pieces and begging to be allowed to become a secret agent for the Hungarian security service, the jovial diplomat spread the prints out on his desk, nodded over them appreciatively and ordered a number of copies "to send to some of my friends who are convinced I'm past it." He even, rumour had it, tried to negotiate a discount for a bulk purchase.

Recklessly tipsy, Lazenby became quite excited when after ten minutes or so of friendly conversation during which the young woman confessed that her name was Marika, envied him his forthcoming visit to Bucharest and complimented him with charming extravagance on his clumsy, ill-phrased Hungarian, she said, in English, "You are sleepy, I think. You wish to go to bed?"

Then she smiled mysteriously, revealing what to Lazenby's heated imagination looked like unnaturally large canine teeth, and slipped away. He downed the rest of his plum brandy and a minute or two later lurched up to his room, quite expecting to find her waiting for him, lying on his bed in a seductive state of undress.

He was disappointed. The jerry-built room was as cheerless and desolate as it had been when he left it. Perhaps Marika planned to come later, he remembered as being his last conscious thought before he stretched out fully clothed on the bed and passed out, to wake up after about two hours with a headache, a desperately dry mouth and still no complaisant Marika. He looked blearily at his watch: it was only a quarter to eleven. It could be asking for trouble to drink tap water, and he had a few bottles of Evian in the boot of the car.

Rather shakily he made his way downstairs, past the reception desk and out of the door. The lobby was deserted but still illuminated and the door unlocked, and the sound of voices came from the restaurant. So Lazenby went round to the Rover, opened the boot and took out one of the precious bottles. He was about to slam the lid closed when it occurred to him to look through the rear window. What he saw made him lower the bootlid with exaggerated care, not bothering to engage the spring lock.

Agnes was sprawled in the back seat fast asleep, with the pathetically scrawny Sandor cradled in her arms, and Lazenby hadn't the heart to disturb them.

He went back to his room, and was, now that he had more or less sobered up, relieved to find that Marika had not had a late change of mind. He locked his door, cleaned his teeth with the aid of a tumbler of Evian water, drank about half a litre of the rest, undressed and tried to banish the memory of his eventful day from his mind.

Further sleep eluded him for what seemed like hours. He puzzled and worried over the enigma of Agnes and her little brother. Not only did they appear to be able to teleport themselves from place to place, but they had lain in wait for him in Cluj, presumably because they had decided in Debrecen that he was a soft touch and a potential long-term meal ticket. How on earth could he be rid of them? Would they continue to dog his path, perhaps even show up at the British Embassy in Budapest?

Then there was the enigmatic Marika, who had definitely behaved in a flirtatious, even seductive manner, and was endowed with unusually long canine teeth. And he hadn't met her until it was almost dark. He was in Transylvania, after all, the home territory of Vlad the Impaler. Could she . . . oh, get hold of yourself, Lazenby. There are no such things as vampires or teleportation. Marika was a perfectly ordinary ethnic Hungarian citizen of Romania, where cosmetic dental work was unavailable to the likes of her, doing her best to make a foreign guest feel welcome.

As for Agnes and Sandor, it was probable that they belonged to an extended gipsy family with ramifications both sides of the border. After being conditioned from infancy to live by their wits it was all too likely that, as soon as they were able to earn, beg or steal enough to support themselves, they had been turned loose to roam free and go to their relatives for help only when they needed it. They might well have uncles or cousins with lorries who could provide long-distance transport . . . and, and . . .

Lazenby did eventually fall into a troubled sleep beset with fantastic dreams, of which he remembered little when he awoke except that he had possessed a communicator and had unavailingly pleaded 'Beam me up, Scotty, please beam me up' as the man he had himself dubbed Dracula tried to sink his teeth into his neck. So vivid was that recollection when morning came that as soon as he was able to drag himself out of bed he went over to the stained mirror above the cracked hand basin and reassured himself that there were no puncture marks on his neck.

He washed and, remembering to retrieve the washbasin

plug he had prudently brought with him, dressed and packed his bag. There was no sign of Marika, and he was served a cup of imitation coffee and a bread roll with bright red jam by way of breakfast by a shuffling crone who cackled at him amiably enough and later presented him with his bill for dinner, room and breakfast. When Lazenby had worked out the rate of exchange he saw that it was even more modest than the ones he had run up in Debrecen.

More than a little apprehensive, he walked out of the hotel and round to the Rover. Its windows and paintwork were sparkling clean, and the hub-caps and windscreen wipers were present and correct. The boot and all the doors were locked, and the toolkit had not been rifled nor had his precious supplies of mineral water been pilfered. Agnes and Sandor did not put in an appearance, and, to his own surprise, it was with relief tinged with some regret that Lazenby drove off, heading for Bucharest by way of Sibiu and Pitesti.

Chapter Five

"Hi! I'm Gosta Lundin from Finland. You're new in town, aren't you? I saw you arrive with Ann and Tom."

"Hello. Ben Lazenby." As he shook hands with the tall, blonde woman, Lazenby realised that this must be the person his colleague and overnight host Tom Dalby had mentioned when telling him about the party he and Ann proposed to take him to that evening. "It's being given by the number two at the Swedish Embassy," Tom explained. "So there'll be a lot of Scandinavians there. Nice people. And you'll probably meet our local sexpot. You're included in the invitation, needless to say. Do you good to socialise after two days in your own company."

Whether or not Ms Lundin was a sexpot as Dalby claimed, she was unquestionably far from being a shrinking violet. Her smile was distinctly voracious, and she clung to his hand a good deal longer than convention required.

Lazenby had been in Bucharest for about six hours, following an uneventful drive from Cluj. He had found the British Embassy without difficulty, arriving just after two. The following hour had been spent mostly with Dalby. He was the Cultural Attaché, like Lazenby a British Council man with diplomatic status, and they were old acquaintances: not quite friends but easy with each other, and had got down to business at once.

The exhibition of British landscape paintings had, according to Dalby, been a great success with the Romanians throughout the month-long run just ended. He showed Lazenby, who had to take his word for it, a number of enthusiastic reviews in the Bucharest press, illustrated with smudgy photographs depicting Dalby himself and his Ambassador in the company of various local notabilities at the opening ceremony. Dalby's view was echoed by his Ambassador when Lazenby was ushered into the presence to pay his respects. The Ambassador's good opinion seemed to be grounded not so much on an informed appraisal of the artistic quality of the paintings as on the impeccable respectability of their subjects. He devoted most of the ten minutes he allowed Lazenby to grumbling belligerently about a visit to his previous post by a group of performance artists sponsored by the British Council, who included a young woman who called herself Cosy Fanny Tutti and whose contribution to the proceedings involved removing all her clothes and being daubed with paint while "squirming and, you know, gyrating about", as His Excellency put it.

Back in Dalby's office, they had discussed the practical arrangements for Lazenby's return journey to Hungary. The paintings were back in the custom-made crates in which they had been flown from London to Bucharest. It was, they agreed, a nuisance that because British Airways could not arrange a charter freight service between the two capitals they had to go by road. However, everything was ready for the off, Dalby explained. The crates had that morning been loaded into two air-conditioned trucks.

"Well, to be quite frank they're refrigerated meat lorries, actually. But the thermostats can be set at any temperature within reason. Sixty degrees Fahrenheit is what the Fine Arts Department insisted on, so that's what you're getting. Bulgarian."

Lazenby goggled at him. "Excuse me, did you say *Bulgarian?*"

"That's right. The Romanians couldn't come up with

anything suitable, but recommended me to try the Bulgarian Embassy. They were enormously helpful, I must say, once I made it clear we could pay in sterling. The lorries duly turned up yesterday."

"From Bulgaria. Good God."

"Oh, I'm sure it'll be fine, Ben. I watched the loading myself. Bit niffy inside, on account of the meat, but the tyres look okay and mechanically they seem to be in quite good nick."

"Tom, are you telling me the paintings are going with a consignment of *meat*?"

"No, no, of course not. But the lorries are *usually* used for meat, fitted out with racks and hooks and so forth, so you'd expect them to pong a bit. Quite clean inside, though. You speak any Bulgarian?

"Me? No. Not a word."

"Pity. The drivers are both Bulgarian. I tried them with English, Romanian and French, but no go. Still, it's not as if you'll be wanting to exchange views with them about the Falklands, is it? And of course you'll have a police escort all the way to the border; the Romanians were very helpful over laying that on."

Filled with foreboding by the prospect of driving to Hungary escorting two meat lorries driven by men who, it seemed, spoke nothing but Bulgarian, Lazenby sat there tired, headachy and increasingly dispirited as Tom Dalby chattered on. Eventually, however, Dalby took pity on him and, after showing him where he could leave the Rover in the Embassy's secure parking compound, drove him to his house. There he was welcomed understandingly by Ann, who took him at once to a blessedly comfortable guest room.

Bathed, shaved, dressed in fresh clothes and having been fed, Lazenby now felt much better; though rather lightheaded. He hadn't seen much of Bucharest, partly because they had driven from the Dalbys' house to the party after nightfall, and the funereally dim street lighting didn't permit more than a shadowy view of drab streets along which a few shabbily dressed pedestrians hurried with heads down, as if seeking refuge from some imminent catastrophe. The Swedish couple's home was bright and cheerful enough, though, and Lazenby decided there were worse things to do after his disconcerting night in Cluj than enjoy the easy camaraderie of perfect strangers who nevertheless welcomed him with the sense of professional solidarity characteristic of off-duty diplomats all over the world.

Gosta Lundin finally released his hand, but only in order to tuck his arm under hers in such a way that it was agreeably squashed by one of her generous breasts. "Come and sit by me and tell me what brings you to this dreary place, Ben," she said, and towed him to a sofa. *En route* he caught Tom Dalby's eye and noted his wink of complicity.

"I'm Tom Dalby's opposite number in Budapest. Here to collect the British paintings that have been on exhibition recently. You may have seen them at the National Gallery."

"Yes, I did. Pleasant, but a bit boring, if you want my honest opinion. Safe, anyhow. Even the Great Leader could hardly object to them. You're staying for a nice long time, I very much hope?"

Lazenby was no longer surprised by the perfect idiomatic English spoken by all the Nordic people he encountered, and wasn't so crass as to compliment her on it. "Sadly, no. I have to head back towards Hungary tomorrow. The journey will take us two days."

Gosta opened her glossy lips and moistened them with her tongue. "Oh, you *lucky* man," she breathed. "To live in Budapest and be able to come and go to Vienna in two or three hours as you please!"

Lazenby realised that he was in danger of being

hypnotised by her mouth, if such a thing was possible, and gave his head a brief shake. "Gosta Lundin, did you say? Isn't that an unusual name for a Finn?"

"Not really. There are Finnish Finns and Swedish Finns, you see, and I'm one of the Swedish kind."

Lazenby nodded. That accounted for the charming, typically Scandinavian lilt in her speech. "Ah, I see. Are you with the Finnish Embassy here?"

"No, no, dear Ben. I'm much too indiscreet to be a diplomat! I'm a journalist. A foreign correspondent for the Finnish News Agency, and I need another drink."

"Sure, I'll get you one. Gin and tonic, is it?" Lazenby had himself asked for plain tonic when his host in welcoming him offered him a drink and ushered him over to a side-table bearing a vast array of bottles. There he was duly equipped with a glass of tonic and urged to help himself from then on.

"Mm, lovely, same as you. Not too much tonic, mind," Gosta said, and ran the tip of her tongue round her lips again as she finally released his arm from its warmly upholstered and by no means uncomfortable prison. After drinking too much both in Debrecen and in Cluj, Lazenby was determined to remain on the wagon throughout the evening, but saw no reason to say so to this Finnish bombshell who seemed to have decided to appropriate him.

That may have been Gosta's intention, but it so turned out that by the time Ben returned to the sofa with fresh supplies the lady was deep in conversation with Ann Dalby, so he was able simply to hand over her drink with a mock bow and be rewarded with a kissing gesture from her luscious lips.

"I noticed you being interviewed by Gosta." The man who attached himself to Lazenby as he moved away with mingled regret and relief sounded Australian, an impression confirmed immediately as he went on. "You want to watch that sheila, mate."

"She's certainly worth watching. Quite a looker," Lazenby said. "She been here long?"

"Long enough to cut a swathe through the available men," the Australian said with a wry smile that suggested he spoke from experience. "My name's Jim East, by the way. And you're Ben Lazenby from Budapest, I'm told. I never know about Finns, do you? They cosy up to the Russians – can't say I blame them for that – but they count as honorary westerners and prefer to run around with us. Nice work, I'd say."

Lazenby shrugged. "Neutrals often have the best of both worlds, and good luck to them."

"All the same, I reckon she's a nark. Always asking questions."

"Well, good grief, she's a journalist. That's what they do for a living." Lazenby spoke rather tartly, having decided that he didn't much take to the Australian, and looked around for a means of escape. East took the hint, raised his glass in an ironic salute and moved off.

The next hour or so passed pleasantly enough. Though Lazenby had never been officially designated as a diplomat before, he had been on the fringes of their world for nearly ten years and had mastered many of the minor social arts called for. These include holding a plate and a full glass simultaneously in one hand while shaking hands with the other, keeping up an endless flow of small talk, and noting who was the senior guest, before whose departure protocol required that nobody could leave even a purely social gathering. The top person that evening was the West German Minister-Counsellor, and when Lazenby saw him go over and thank his hostess, closely tailed by his Danish counterpart, he knew it meant the party was about to break up.

He was curious to see whether Gosta Lundin had either come with an escort or acquired one during the course of the evening, and was a little surprised when she left alone, but not without a wave to him: a wave accompanied by another eloquent kissing gesture. Then he put her out of his mind in the flurry of thanks and farewells.

Ann Dalby was driving and he sat beside her in the front passenger seat while her husband sprawled, only slightly the worse for wear, in the back. They all chatted for a while in a desultory way, until Ann glanced across at Lazenby and asked him the question he'd been expecting.

"Well, what did you make of Gosta Lundin?"

"A bit overpowering, I must say. She's obviously no fool, though."

"She certainly isn't. She managed to get an interview with Ceauşescu recently for her agency in Finland and they've sold it on to all manner of papers, it seems. Tom and I read it ourselves in the Observer last week. Cultural Section's copy arrives at the Embassy best part of a week late and Tom brings it home for the weekend, don't you, Tom?"

Tom grunted assent, then yawned noisily, obviously content to leave the conversation to the others.

"When I complimented her on it she said it was appearing in the New York Times, the International Herald Tribune, and Le Monde. In her own English and French translations, I shouldn't wonder. Yup. There's no doubt Gosta's built up a solid reputation in a profession still dominated by you lot."

"Well, I'm truly staggered." Lazenby could hardly credit what he'd just heard. Could the predatory, almost vulgarly seductive woman who had snuggled up to him more or less on sight really be a respected journalist? One, moreover, who had contrived to secure an exclusive interview with the notoriously autocratic and suspicious megalomaniac Ceauşescu? And whose work enjoyed such impressive international marketability? The notion was so difficult for him to accept that he was briefly tempted to suspect, absurdly, that the "Gosta Lundin" he had encountered was an impostor.

"Anyway," Ann Dalby went on, "what all this is in aid of is that Gosta asked me how you might react to the idea of giving her a lift to Budapest tomorrow."

Chapter Six

Too tired to take in the possible implications of what Ann Dalby had proposed, Lazenby went to his third unfamiliar bed in three nights leaving his host and hostess still debating the propriety of Gosta Lundin's request to go with Lazenby in his car to Budapest.

Tom had been less surprised by it than Lazenby; but then he had met her many times and was impressed by her standing in her profession. He also knew how difficult it was for a foreigner without diplomatic status to get about rural Romania, and Gosta had, it seemed, waxed eloquent to Ann in making her request.

She had admitted to Ann that she could perfectly easily go by air to Budapest, but explained that the point was not to arrive so much as to observe what could be seen on the way. As soon as she had heard about Lazenby's proposed journey, therefore, Gosta had seen it as a heaven-sent opportunity for her to invite herself along in order to gather material for a feature article comparing and contrasting life in the Romanian countryside with that in Eastern Hungary. Presumably she had felt that as a fan of hers Ann would be a persuasive go-between, as indeed she turned out to be.

Her husband was not unsympathetic, but felt that Gosta was being unreasonable in proposing to travel as a passenger in a car bearing diplomatic plates which identified it as belonging to an envoy from a NATO country. What would be acceptable on a recreational local drive would not appear to be anything like as innocent in the case of a long-distance official journey. The fact that Lazenby's car and two large articulated lorries were to be under Romanian police escort as far as the border made the whole idea so much the worse in Dalby's view.

By breakfast time, however, Tom had, as a good bureaucrat, decided to pass the buck to Lazenby, who to his own surprise had slept like a top. "I know what'll happen if I ask my Head of Chancery for his agreement. He'd squash the idea right away: they're all twitchy at the Embassy now over Carrington's resignation and this Falklands task force business. So I daren't so much as even mention it. On the other hand, there isn't any need for me to. You see, the moment you and the trucks get under way, my responsibility ends and yours begins. So as I see it, it's absolutely up to you to decide whether to take Gosta along with you or not."

Lazenby looked at him reproachfully over a spoonful of muesli. "Be reasonable, Tom. You spelt out all the obvious objections yourself last night. How can I take her, for heaven's sake? I know you and Ann both vouch for her, but I've hardly met the woman. She may be a hotshot journalist, but if I turn up on the Hungarian side of the border with her as excess baggage I'm quite likely to find myself in the shit there."

"Excess baggage! I say, that's rather a neat description of our Gosta. I must say I do see your point. Tell you what, leave her this side, then. Take her as far as Arad. You're due to spend the night there. Drop her at the railway station. She can get a train to Budapest from there, and talk her own way into Hungary. I'm sure she has a valid visa as an accredited journalist there too. Not to mention several other central European and Balkan countries."

"Look, Tom, I don't *need* this. Anyway, I thought we were due to move off at about eleven. Surely Gosta Lundin isn't sitting somewhere with her bag packed waiting for a phone call at this late stage? No, I'm sorry if you think I'm letting you down, Ann, but it just isn't on, you know."

About two hours later, Lazenby stood with Dalby outside the back of the National Art Museum, looking apprehensively at two Bulgarian-registered juggernauts with international TIR plates. Their engines were running and their drivers, thickset, unshaven men, were sitting in the cabs looking morose.

"Don't they even have, what do you call them, driver's mates? What happens if one of them breaks down?"

"Calm down, Ben," Dalby said soothingly, pointing to a neat blue police car beside which two smartly uniformed men were standing smoking cigarettes. "If anything *were* to go amiss, your minders would take care of everything. But it won't happen. Those drivers spend their lives barrelling all over the continent and they know the score."

"Yes, but how the blazes do you imagine I'm going to *communicate* with them? In sign language?"

"You speak German or Russian?"

"German a bit. Russian not a word."

"I wouldn't mind betting they speak Russian, but I couldn't try that with them, because I don't know any either. Or German. Why don't you have a go?"

Lazenby shrugged, but walked over to the nearest lorry and attempted an ingratiating smile. The driver surveyed him gloomily.

"*Guten Morgen*" he said and to his surprise the man growled back at him. It sounded vaguely like "*Morgen*", and Ben was emboldened to continue.

"*Sie sprechen Deutsch?*

"*Bisschen.*"

A little. Thank God for that. Lazenby beamed. "*Ich auch,*" he said, nodding and smiling like an idiot before turning away and rejoining Dalby.

"Well, it seems he does speak a bit of German, at least."

"Great. You'll be fine then, won't you? Well, your own car's been tanked up, tyres, oil and water checked and so forth, so you're all set. Now remember, you'll be taking the direct route to Budapest from Sibiu onwards, not the one you came in by, so the border town this side is Arad, not Oradea. You should arrive there well before dark. The Arad fuzz will meet you just outside the town, where those chaps over there will make their farewells to you and turn back. The locals will pilot you to the hotel where a room's been booked in your name, mount a guard over the lorries overnight, and escort you to the actual border first thing in the morning. I understand the drivers always sleep in their cabs – "

"Hi, boys! Looks as if I'm just in time."

Both men turned and gaped at Gosta Lundin, looking stylish but workmanlike in designer jeans and a plaid shirt, her blonde hair tied back into a ponytail with a bit of ribbon. She was approaching jauntily, carrying a small suitcase and looking the picture of vigorous health, like an advertisement for Vitamin C tablets.

Dalby was the first to address her. "Gosta, what on earth . . .? Didn't Ann ring you to explain?"

"Oh yah, she rang. That's how I found out when you're due to leave, dear Ben. So I came anyway."

Lazenby took a deep breath. "Listen, Gosta, I'm sorry, but I simply can't take you."

"They've moved off. You ought to know that he's got a passenger. A woman."

"Has he indeed. What does she look like?"

"Tall, blonde, in her thirties, I'd say. The thing is, the Englishman didn't seem to be at all keen to take her. I got the impression that the other one had to talk him into it. I mean the one from the British Embassy who's been in charge of the exhibition here."

"I see. All right, leave it with me."

The state security officer put the telephone down and resumed his ostensible duties as doorkeeper at the National Art Gallery in Bucharest, while the man to whom he had been speaking sat at his headquarters desk, thoughtfully picking his teeth with a matchstick while staring unseeingly at his own phone. After a while he picked up the receiver again and pressed one of the three buttons on the instrument. He heard a purring sound very briefly before the person at the other end of the line responded.

"Yes?"

"It seems our bird is planning to leave the nest under British diplomatic protection. She's currently in a car driven by their so-called Cultural Attaché from Budapest, and they're heading in that direction."

"I see. Not a bad idea. I hope she has the egg with her. Arrange to have an eye kept on her to make sure she doesn't drop it into the wrong hands on the way."

"Are you very mad at me, dear Ben?"

Lazenby kept his eyes sullenly on the road. "Yes. And I'm not your dear Ben."

"But everything's going so well! The men in the police car saluted us when we got in, and Tom Dalby waved so cheerfully as we left."

Lazenby reached down and brusquely removed Gosta's hand from his thigh. "Tom Dalby has no reason *not* to be cheerful. You're not his responsibility."

"Ooh, look! There's another set of traffic lights with a policeman waving us through! Wow, you must be even more important than I thought."

In spite of himself Lazenby was impressed by the slickness of the operation mounted by the Romanian police, and made a mental note to speak in pointedly glowing terms about it to Dracula. At every major intersection in the Bucharest metropolitan area a Romanian policeman had been posted to ensure that Lazenby's cavalcade had priority, and most of them saluted respectfully as the Rover swept by. Lazenby felt that he could hardly salute back, but he did incline his head graciously as he passed, while Gosta waved and, Lazenby suspected, blew kisses.

He maintained an ill-tempered silence for the better part of an hour, fiddling with the radio and merely grunting whenever Gosta said anything. The first part of the journey followed the route he had traversed on the way into Budapest the previous day, and the countryside was no more interesting than he had found it then, so out of growing boredom and an uncomfortable feeling that he was being childish, Lazenby eventually weakened and spoke to his passenger.

"Listen, Gosta. I'm only taking you as far as Arad, you know. And that's not negotiable. We're supposed to arrive there at about four, and from there on you must make your own arrangements. Tom says there are trains to Budapest, and no doubt the hotel people can fix you up with a taxi to the station. I couldn't drive you there even if I wanted to, you see. I've got to stay with the lorries."

"Yes, of course," she said meekly. "I'm very sorry to be such a nuisance to you, Ben."

"Yes, well, it's a bit late for that now. Hadn't you better take the opportunity to make some notes? For your article?"

"Article? Oh, yah."

"Will you be writing anything about the gipsies?"

Gosta Lundin didn't respond for a while, and Lazenby glanced sideways at her. She had a strange expression on her face. "Gipsies? Why do you ask such a thing?"

"Well, they have a pretty rough time of it in Hungary, and I can't imagine it's much different for them here. I suppose I mentioned them because I had a curious experience the day before yesterday, while I was on my way to Bucharest."

"Tell me about it." Gosta's manner had changed. She was no longer winsomely apologetic or flirtatious, but quietly attentive, as if she really wanted to hear what he had to say. Lazenby turned his head briefly to look at her properly. Seeing her gazing intently at him, he gave a little shrug as he returned his attention to the road ahead, then told her briefly about his encounter with the two children outside the Debrecen University buildings, and of his astonishment when they turned up again outside the hotel in Cluj.

Gosta sat very still as he described how Agnes had accounted for their seemingly miraculous apparition there, and reached over and briefly squeezed his thigh when he mentioned that he had given her some American dollars. This time, the gesture communicated itself as being friendly and impulsive rather than calculated, and she withdrew her hand after a few seconds. He decided not to mention leaving one door of his car unlocked and finding Agnes and her brother asleep inside it late in the evening.

"To tell you the truth, I was half expecting them to show up at the Art Gallery this morning, but you did instead." Lazenby's humour had improved as he was telling his story, and he infused some cordiality into his voice as he brought it to an end.

"It was kind of you to give them money." Gosta's voice was flat, and she sounded almost melancholy.

"Oh, that was nothing. But I'm still at a loss to know how they found out I was going to Cluj, and how in the world they contrived to arrive there before me."

"They probably followed you from Debrecen and saw you heading for the border. It was an intelligent guess that you would at least stop for a meal in Cluj, that's all. And I expect they were telling the truth about how they travelled. The gipsies know ways of by-passing border controls."

"So I've gathered. You seem to know a lot about them."

"I've . . . made a study."

"So, will you mention them in this famous article?"

To Lazenby's surprise Gosta Lundin heaved a sigh. "No, I don't think that would do any good. I hope I can do more to help them in other ways." She leant forward in her seat and peered ahead. "What's happening?" The lorry in front of them was slowing down decisively. Tucked in as they were behind it, Lazenby couldn't see the police car leading them, but as the lorry came to a halt and he followed suit, he could see that they had come to a roadside restaurant. Almost immediately, one of the two police officers escorting them approached on foot with a smile.

"This Rimlicu Vilcea. We take liddle break," he said. "Ten, fifteen minutes only."

Lazenby nodded and smiled agreement, got out of the car and stretched luxuriously as he looked around him. They had left the plain, and the view ahead was of the hills on either side of the valley of the River Oltul, beside which they would be climbing slowly before reaching a pass after which he knew they would descend again into Sibiu.

The lavatory facilities at the restaurant were basic, but reasonably clean and very welcome. The coffee was barely drinkable, but the bread rolls were still warm, and Lazenby ate two. The two policemen were being fussed over at a table well away from the one to which he and Gosta had been directed, and the Bulgarian drivers were at the counter. The only other customer in the place was a nondescript middle-aged man in a suit, reading a newspaper. After a while the English-speaking escort wandered over, cigarette in hand. "Okay we go now?"

"Yes, good. Thank you." Lazenby stood, and drew

Gosta's chair back for her as she followed suit. Though they had exchanged only small talk over their coffee and rolls, she had continued to be quiet and serious, as though still brooding over his story about the gipsy children. They obediently followed the Romanian policeman towards the door with the lorry drivers falling in behind, while his colleague, who seemed by the look of his uniform to be the more senior of the two, made off in the direction of the lavatory. Lazenby felt encouraged by this indication of common humanity as he stepped outside, squared his shoulders and took a deep breath of the clean-smelling air, such a relief after the polluted atmosphere of Bucharest.

Then he noticed that one of his shoelaces was undone, murmured "Go ahead, I'll catch you up," to Gosta and stooped to re-tie it. Had he not done so, he wouldn't have caught sight through one of the restaurant windows of the senior police officer in close conversation with the man in the suit.

Chapter Seven

When the Romanian police car, the two juggernauts and the Rover were once again under way it was Lazenby's turn to brood: about the man inside the restaurant. Unfortunately there was nothing mysterious about him. Dressed in a suit like that he had to be some kind of official, and the fact that the police officers had ignored him until they assumed that the two Bulgarians, the British diplomat and his glamorous companion were safely back in their vehicles made it a very safe bet that he had been sent there to check up on Lazenby's relationship with Gosta.

As she had pointed out a couple of hours earlier, neither their police escort nor the little group of gallery officials who had been present to wave them farewell as they set off had seemed to react to her arrival on the scene. Nor did anyone notice – at least ostensibly – Lazenby's discreetly subdued but intense irritation as he tried and failed to turn her away. When Gosta simply gave him a brilliant smile, opened the passenger door and sat down, he should have ordered her out and if necessary physically ejected her from the car. He now saw that all too clearly, and silently cursed the Dalbys. It was all their fault. Not only had Ann listened to Gosta in the first place, but when this bloody woman didn't take no for an answer and forced her way into the car Tom told him quietly but firmly not to create a scene, and then had the cheek to put her suitcase on the back seat and close the door for her.

It had all been done quickly and without overt fuss, but

it now dawned on Lazenby that it was in the highest degree unlikely that none of the witnesses had been curious about the little argument beside the Rover. He felt himself flushing with embarrassment, and his heart pounding as apprehension sent the adrenalin surging through his bloodstream. God, how could he – and Tom – have been so naive! Their Romanian police escorts – not to mention the policemen so obligingly holding up the traffic for them at each intersection – were obviously in radio contact with their superiors. They in turn would have been alerted by whichever of the gallery officials was a member of the security service and informed that the British exhibition material in transit to Budapest was being escorted not only by a properly accredited male diplomat but also by a woman.

Ceaușescu's security service undoubtedly monitored the movements of all westerners, especially when they ventured outside Bucharest city limits. That went for the rare tourists too, and they would certainly keep an eye on "friendly neutrals" such as Finns. As a well-known journalist, Gosta Lundin was conspicuous in the expatriate community. Even if he'd never seen her before, the man in the restaurant would have been told who she was and what she did for a living. That she had a certain reputation among the male members of the western community would not have escaped the attention of the Romanian spooks either, so it was quite likely that he also knew what she did in her spare time and with whom.

Well, he'd told her he would give her a lift to Arad, and much as he was tempted to abandon her at Sibiu, he wouldn't go back on his word. If challenged when they reached Arad he would simply state the truth: that he had been asked to give Ms Lundin a lift as far as there, and knew of no reason why he should not have done so. As for Gosta, she'd got herself into this and could bloody well brazen herself out of it again. She presumably knew whether or not she was in breach of Romanian law, and could reasonably argue that if she were up to no good she'd hardly set about it by joining anything so conspicuous as a road convoy under police escort. This thought comforted Lazenby somewhat.

His anxieties were further mitigated when he reminded himself that there was little love lost between the so-called "fraternal" socialist governments of Romania and of Hungary. The more he thought about it, the more improbable it seemed that word of his indiscretion would reach the Hungarian authorities. Even if they did get to hear about it, they'd most likely be only mildly interested, and note it without comment on his dossier. Giving a lady a lift was, after all, less out of the ordinary than Comrade Nagy's unauthorised impromptu visit to his brother-in-law the priest on the way to Debrecen. No, any problem that might arise would be Gosta's, not his. Damn it all, the chap in the restaurant might conceivably be the manager of the place, discussing who should pay for their refreshments, because it hadn't occurred to Lazenby to do so.

He didn't really believe that, but by the time he noticed a sign announcing that the scattering of houses on either side of the road was called Cozia he was disposed to make conversation again. Gosta had been silent, perhaps sensing that he was having a mental wrestling match with himself, perhaps enjoying the scenery. The road offered frequent views of the river and of the Carpathian mountains on either side.

"Spectacular, isn't it?"

"Sorry?"

"The scenery. I saw it when I was coming from the other direction yesterday on my way to Bucharest. I was impressed then, and I still am."

"Oh. Yah. You know some of the peaks are over two thousand metres? The one ahead on the left must be at least that high."

"Still capped with snow in April. Be like that for another month or so, I imagine. I wouldn't like to be lost in this sort of country any time, least of all in winter."

"No."

Lazenby decided to take the bull by the horns. "Gosta, you do realise that the Romanians are sure to have checked up on your identity? It doesn't bother me," he lied bravely, "but aren't you supposed to get permission to travel so far out of Bucharest?"

She shrugged with apparent nonchalance, but Lazenby had the firm impression that she was uneasy. "Well, yes, that's so technically, but they won't bother me while I'm with you. Perhaps after Arad, but I've talked myself into and out of a good many tricky situations in the past. I have valid exit/re-entry permits for both Romania and Hungary, so I'm sure they'll let me on the international train. I speak Romanian, and if anyone tries to stop me I shall frighten him by letting him know that I'm personally acquainted with Ceauşescu. I won't mention that when I'm on the Hungarian side of the border, of course."

She sounded both gallant and scared, almost like a child pretending not to be afraid of the dark, and Lazenby was touched in spite of himself. He was also slightly puzzled. Was this the way a tough, resourceful lady and seasoned international journalist should react to the possibility of a mere bureaucratic tangle at Arad railway station likely to result at worst in a ritual ticking-off from the Romanians?

He decided he liked her well enough to ask her the question he had been formulating in his mind for some time. "Gosta, what's the real reason why you wanted so much to come with me? It wasn't a sudden impulse, was it? Nor to collect material for a routine feature article."

Her reply startled him. "Dear Ben, is there a chance your car has been bugged?"

He looked at her, then away again as the car swerved

a little too close to the low barrier at the side of the road for comfort. The glimpse he'd had of her face persuaded him that it was a serious question deserving a straight answer.

"Not likely at all, in my opinion. The Romanians could have got at it in Cluj, but it was parked last night in the secure Embassy compound in Bucharest and will have been routinely swept by one of our technical security people. And nobody's touched it except us today."

"What about while we were in the restaurant?"

"It was locked, Gosta. And we weren't away from it long enough to allow for that kind of operation. No, you can talk freely, I'm sure. And I promise on my personal honour that I'll respect any confidences you care to share."

"I have no option. And I must trust you if I want you to help me. You were kind to the gipsy children, that's something. You wouldn't want them to die."

"To *die*? What on earth are you talking about?"

"Listen carefully, Ben, and don't interrupt. You're right about one thing; I did make up the story about writing an article. When I heard you were going to be driving to Hungary today I decided that I must come with you if at all possible. You see, it's vital that I get something out of Romania, and you could give me diplomatic protection – no, *please* don't say anything until I've finished . . ."

She sat in silence for a couple of minutes, then launched into a long but coherent story that Lazenby had no wish to interrupt. It was seemingly only his casual reference to his experiences with Agnes and Sandor that persuaded Gosta to confide in him. She told him that she had met and talked at length to a number of Romanian dissidents in Budapest, and been provided with some hard facts and figures about Ceauşescu's megalomaniac insistence on erasing the last surviving vestiges of individualism by ordering the bulldozing of whole towns and villages.

Traditional communities were being ruthlessly broken up, with people being forcibly dispersed and relocated in dismal barracks far away. That was dreadful enough, but the policy as such was no secret. It wasn't however all that was being planned in the name of socialist progress.

Gosta was informed by her contacts that the way in which Ceauşescu and his toadies intended to deal with the matter of the gipsies was by copying, in conditions of the utmost secrecy, Hitler's Final Solution. They were simply to disappear: old and young men, women, children and babies were to be rounded up and put to death. Gosta was properly sceptical, and told the dissidents that without convincing evidence it was out of the question for her to drag the matter into the open.

Then, quite by coincidence, her long-standing request to be permitted to interview Nicolae Ceauşescu himself was approved, and she was required to submit a list of questions in advance, in English. This she did, taking care to make them prudently anodyne; and in due course she was summoned to the presidential palace for an audience with the great man.

"Well, the great day arrived, and turned out to be a truly extraordinary experience," she told Lazenby as they left the Carpathians behind them, were waved through the outskirts of Sibiu by yet more policemen and headed towards Sebes where they would strike due west. "When I arrived at the presidential palace they took away everything I had with me. Bag, camera, tape recorder, everything. Then would you believe it, I was, what's the expression, strip-searched, and I mean thoroughly, by a frightful woman security guard before I was allowed to put my clothes on again." Gosta shuddered at the recollection.

"It was *horrible*, Ben. And the worst thing was that I'm sure she was enjoying humiliating me. Anyway, after that I was taken through various rooms that looked like something out of an old Cecil B. de Mille movie. Marble floors, gold leaf everywhere, grand but vulgar in a way I can't really describe. The staff were dressed up in amazing uniforms, too, with more and more medals and epaulettes and so on as we got nearer to the boss. I could see those awful beady red eyes of security cameras tracking my every move, until we came to a pair of huge double doors that opened as if by magic. I went into Ceauşescu's study. It's absolutely *colossal*, Ben. Red draperies trimmed with gold at the windows, a huge desk and all the furniture in a sort of mad Third Empire style. And there he was, facing me from across a carpet the size of a football pitch."

"God almighty. What does he look like in the flesh?"

"Well, fleshy. Plump and oily-looking, but quite well dressed. He had a woman interpreter there, who dealt with the introductory courtesies very expertly in excellent English, much better than mine. I thought it wise not to let on that I understand Romanian. Then he waved me to an absurd little gilt chair, and the interpreter handed me a copy of the questions I'd submitted, with written replies. "Tell her to stick to the text in her article. Anything I say in conversation is off the record. Not for publication", I heard Ceauşescu murmur to her, and she translated what he said accurately. Well, I glanced through the replies, which were as turgid and boring as you'd expect, then I brightly enquired if His Excellency would be good enough to enlarge – not for publication, of course – on some topics known to be close to his heart." Gosta paused and closed her eyes for a moment before continuing.

"I can tell you that the interpreter began by passing on more or less everything Ceauşescu said, but when I moved on from banalities to potentially touchy subjects such as the so-called rural modernisation programme she became more and more uneasy. Ceauşescu got more and more excited, and she translated only the less extreme remarks. I could see that he was losing control of himself, which needless to say I was very pleased about, so in all apparent innocence, I asked him *in Romanian* how the ethnic minorities such as the Hungarians and the gipsies would be affected by the programme, and Ceauşescu seemed to go berserk. I couldn't understand much of what he was practically screaming, and the interpreter didn't even attempt to enlighten me. I was fascinated of course, but beginning to get a bit scared; but then a man in an ordinary suit hurried into the room and said something to Ceauşescu very quietly. I've no idea what it was, but it stopped him in his tracks. He blinked a lot, and had a dazed look on his face. Then the man whispered something to the interpreter, who had been sitting there obviously terrified, and she told me that unfortunately urgent affairs of state made it necessary for the interview to be brought to an end. I wasn't all that sorry, believe me."

"Oh, I do indeed," Lazenby said fervently. "So what happened after that?"

"Well, this guy showed me out of the room and took me to a small office, where he worked quite hard at charming me. He spoke good English, and explained that the Great Leader had been under considerable strain recently. Then he gave me a glass of excellent red wine – which I needed after that – and turned on the heat. He made it very plain to me that my continued accreditation in Romania would depend on how faithfully anything I wrote about the interview followed the approved script, avoiding what he described as anything of a personal nature. Then he escorted me to the entrance, where I got my belongings back, and I drove myself back to my apartment. I work from there too. You can imagine that I was excited and confused. Frustrated, too, because I didn't see how I could make use of the amazing material I'd gathered."

She exhaled loudly and rested her hand briefly on

Lazenby's again. "Anyway, here comes the best bit. It wasn't until I got home that I discovered that somebody at the palace had put a cassette tape in my shoulder bag."

Chapter Eight

After delivering her punch line Gosta fell silent as they came to the outskirts of Birzava and the convoy was waved through the small town by traffic policemen who, like their colleagues elsewhere, saluted respectfully as they drove by.

Lazenby waited patiently for her to continue her story until they were clear of the built-up area, but then thought it was time to remind her that they were due to part company quite soon. "It can't be far to Arad now. We have perhaps half an hour of privacy left. I thank you for telling me all this fascinating stuff, Gosta, and I admire what you're doing. I'm right, am I, in assuming that the tape is a recording of Ceauşescu's genocidal rantings and that you're going to try to smuggle it out?"

"Yes, Ben. I made a copy of it, of course, and left it in safe hands, but it wouldn't stand up to expert technical analysis as the original will."

"The interview as you wrote it up seems to have impressed a lot of people in Europe and America, yet the Romanian authorities haven't made any complaint I take it?"

"No. Because I did stick to the approved script. It was published and my agency was able to sell it on to so many papers partly because he so rarely gives interviews at all. For foreign consumption I mean. The Romanian party newspapers publish his pictures every day and carry endless reports of his speeches, needless to say. I did try very subtly to make some, how shall I say, sly little points which might have got across to some readers, and they seem not to have been noticed here. Or perhaps they were, but were glossed over by translators too terrified of him to draw attention to them."

Lazenby sighed and shook his head, more sorrowful than angry. "And if I had been fool enough to agree to take you over the border you'd have kept me in blissful ignorance about your contraband, I suppose."

"Yes. It would have been safer that way. You have a very open face, you know. But Ben, I'd do anything to persuade you to change your mind even now and take me."

"Anything?" He didn't in the least intend the sexual innuendo commonly loading the one-word question when addressed by a man to an attractive woman, being interested only in the strength of her resolve; but the silence that followed for a few seconds made him painfully aware that she must have misinterpreted him, and he felt mortified.

"If you mean would I make love with you, yes, of course I would. I think it would be very nice and a lot of fun, actually." Gosta's light-hearted answer came as a relief and a surprise, but it also replaced Lazenby's remorse with a moment of ill-considered indignation.

"Good grief, woman, I'm not about to risk being declared *persona non grata* for the sake of a fuck, however enjoyable." As soon as he had blurted the words out he remembered that he had come rather close to doing just that with Marika the receptionist at the hotel in Cluj, and that the only reason he hadn't was that she'd failed to show up at his room. Blushing with shame, he hastened to try to make amends.

"I'm sorry, Gosta. I shouldn't have put it like that. It was crude and unnecessary, and you must be under great strain anyway. Listen, I've already said I admire you, I've come to respect you, and I do also think you're extremely attractive. Please believe me: in other circumstances I'd consider it a privilege to make love with you, but not as part of a bargain of that kind."

Gosta reached over and squeezed the hand he was resting loosely on the gear lever. "Well, thank you for saying that. And I do realise now that I was hoping too much of you. Okay. I'll take the train from Arad to Budapest and meet you there after we've both arrived safely. Then we'll celebrate, and perhaps end up in bed all the same. Thank you anyway for bringing me this far." Gosta leant over and kissed him on the cheek; the touch of her lips was like an electric shock.

More than once during the next few minutes Lazenby was on the point of changing his mind about abandoning Gosta at Arad, but prudence kept his mouth shut and before long the right turn lights on the lorry he was following began to flash. Ahead he was able to see the police car and the lead lorry leave the road and turn into the spacious car park of a modern three-storey hotel that looked as if it might rate two or even three stars in the West. He followed the second lorry in, and soon noticed and obeyed the hand signals of a policeman waving him towards a parking space beside the main entrance.

"So, I must say *au revoir*, dear Ben," Gosta said as he applied the hand-brake and switched off the ignition. "I'll just go inside and ask the hotel people about train times and get them to arrange a taxi for me. You will be busy with your policemen. Thank you again for everything."

"Gosta – forgive me, but I must know. You haven't hidden the tape somewhere in my car, have you?"

Her eyes half closed and a sad little smile on her lips, Gosta shook her head. "No, Ben. I swear that I haven't. But I'm truly grateful to you all the same." Then she put one hand behind his head, leaned over and kissed him full on the mouth for two long seconds before releasing him and opening the passenger door. "Have a good trip for the rest of the way. And please do what you can for the gipsies."

He scrambled out and retrieved her suitcase from the back seat for her. She looked at the locks closely for a moment and then up at him with a rueful smile. "Well, well. Such a surprise. You know, Ben, this has been opened since this morning. I thought it might be tampered with, so I set a little trap. It must have been at the restaurant where we stopped. Just their suspicious natures, I guess. Well, they won't have found anything interesting inside. Bye bye, Ben. See you in Budapest."

Then he saw only her shapely back as, head held high and hips swinging bravely, she went into the hotel carrying her suitcase. Lazenby stood watching her, feeling a complete shit.

As Gosta had predicted, Lazenby's policemen did demand most of his attention during the following half-hour. The officers who had escorted the convoy from Bucharest took their leave with formal courtesy after introducing by name Lieutenant Enescu from Arad police headquarters.

Enescu was a sallow, youngish man, dandified in manner and appearance and with a good command of slightly off-beat English laced with French. Referring to himself in the third person, he explained that his men would mount guard over the lorries "most diligently" throughout the night. In the morning Enescu would personally lead the convoy to a nearby filling station which sold both diesel fuel and premium grade petrol, and thence to the border control point.

"A short distance only, maybe thirty, thirty-five kilometres about. There will be two police *voitures*, that of Enescu in the front, and another one at the backside. You will travel alone, sir?"

"Oh yes, Lieutenant. Absolutely."

Enescu nodded, his face expressionless. "Is good so, *n'est ce pas?*"

"Lieutenant, I'm a little worried about the truck drivers. I think they plan to sleep in their cabs, but where will they eat, and wash, and so forth?"

"They go, they stay with their *camions*, it makes nothing to Enescu." He waved vaguely in a westerly direction. "They know Arad. There are bars, they have money."

"Do they?" Even as Lazenby spoke, one of the Bulgarians clambered down from his juggernaut and trudged towards him, pulling on a plastic leather-look blouson and with a look of glum distaste on his stubbly face. He locked the cab door after him, but a continuing rumble testified to the fact that the air-conditioning machinery was still running.

"*Bleib hier bis morgen*", he growled, as though daring Lazenby to disagree.

"*Ja. Vielen Dank.*" Lazenby looked at the Romanian police officer. "At what time are we due to move off tomorrow, Lieutenant? A Hungarian official is to meet us on his side of the frontier at ten-thirty."

A mirthless smile flittered over Enescu's face, and he shrugged. "Enescu will come at eight hours. We move perhaps at eight-thirty. Clear Romania *douane* one hour most after then." He shrugged again and turned his gaze heavenward, as if to imply that he neither knew nor cared what kind of mess the Hungarians would make of the arrangements on their side.

Lazenby smiled weakly at the squat Bulgarian, and edged to one side to keep him downwind. He decided to think of him as Boris and his colleague as Ivan. "*Ja. Bis morgen fruh. Um acht Uhr. Danke. Viel Vergnug.*" Boris the driver belched consideringly, as if in wonderment at the idea that anyone could think of having a good time in such a benighted spot, and then lumbered off, to be joined by Ivan. Lazenby thought it unlikely that they would find a wedding party going on in town, or be invited after the example of Comrade Nagy to join in the festivities if they did.

"Well, thank you, Lieutenant Enescu. I should like to compliment you and your Bucharest colleagues. All the arrangements made for the transportation by road of this important art exhibition have been most efficient. Well, I shall go and check in now, dine in the hotel and be ready to leave by eight tomorrow morning. Thank you again, Lieutenant. See you in the morning, then."

"Enescu goes with you inside." Lazenby's heart sank. For all his slightly comic manner of speech, there was something vaguely menacing about the man. It would be frightful if he was going to be stuck with his company and have to make conversation until bedtime. Even Dracula would be preferable as a dinner companion.

Throughout his negotiations with the police and the Bulgarians, Lazenby had continued to feel guilty and concerned about Gosta, and he was sure he would have noticed if she had left the hotel again. But there was no sign of her in the lobby, which smelt a little of cabbage, and it was clearly not the moment to enquire about her.

One good thing at least soon became clear. It turned out that his new minder had meant nothing more by his ominous remark than that he wanted to usher Lazenby through the process of registration, and sneak a look at the first floor room they were shown to with some ceremony. Once there, Lieutenant Enescu looked round it, nodded in satisfaction and said "My word! *De grand luxe, n'est ce pas?*"

It wasn't, but Lazenby agreed with him volubly all the same, and to his great relief Enescu shook him solemnly by the hand, nodded curtly and went out of the room. It was just after four in the afternoon. "Good evening," he said, turning in the open doorway. "Enescu will leave you and go back tomorrow."

Chapter Nine

Left to himself, Lazenby first opened his own suitcase, which unlike Gosta's had been locked in the boot of the Rover all day. There was nothing in it but clothes, washing gear and other innocent belongings, and he hadn't bothered to employ any of the usual simple tell-tales, such as a length of cotton placed in such a way that it would break if the contents were disturbed. Nevertheless, as far as he could see, nothing had been touched. In any case, if Romanian security had been through his luggage as well as Gosta's during their refreshment stop they would have had to work fearsomely fast, and be disappointed a second time for their pains.

He had brought only his diplomatic ID card, passport and money with him from Hungary, and carried all those on his person. There were some odds and ends in his wallet as well as his emergency supply of hard currency, Hungarian forints and Romanian lei: an organ donor card, his British driving licence, his American Express card, a scrap of paper on which he'd scribbled a few important telephone numbers, and a photograph of his former wife that he looked at less and less frequently as time passed. His file of official correspondence about the exhibition, which contained nothing remotely sensitive, was in any event in the briefcase that he had kept by his side all day, along with the receipts from the restaurant in Debrecen and the hotels there and in Cluj. Lazenby looked round the unremarkable room which Lieutenant Enescu had admired so exuberantly. It was a distinct improvement on the one he had occupied in Cluj, but much less comfortably furnished than the suite that Viktor Szekacs had reserved for him at the Golden Ox in Debrecen. It was at the front of the building, which faced south, and from the grimy window he had a view of most of the hotel car park. His own car was visible below, just to the left of the rudimentary driveway from the main road about fifty metres away, while the two meat transporters were parked well over to the right, tucked in beside a concrete and wire boundary fence. Nearby was a police car with one door wide open, revealing one of Enescu's finest chewing on something half-wrapped in paper, and a companion dimly visible beyond him.

Nothing of the town of Arad could be seen from his window, though it couldn't be far away, and the road was tinted dusty gold in the last glow of the setting sun.

It ought to have been a satisfying moment for Lazenby: he had almost completed his mission, and had every reason to appreciate the co-operation of the Romanian authorities whose efficiency in arranging such a trouble-free journey for him and the cargo in his charge did them much credit. It was impossible to imagine the British police laying on an escort for a couple of truckloads of Hungarian artefacts *en route* from, say, Manchester to France via Dover.

Yet Gosta had claimed that her suitcase had been surreptitiously opened and searched. Well, fair enough, perhaps. She'd more or less forced her way on board as an unauthorised passenger on an officially escorted road convoy. The Romanians would certainly have made it their business to identify her, and might well have assumed that he, Lazenby, planned to take her over the border with him.

The important question was whether or not the security authorities were aware of the existence of a hot potato in the form of a tape recording of Ceauşescu's voice, which must have been passed to Gosta by a well-placed undercover dissident sympathiser in the dictator's immediate entourage, and that it was in Gosta's possession. If they were, then obviously they would have suspected at once that she was attempting to smuggle it out of the country. Even if they weren't, they would obviously interest themselves in the movements of a well-known Finnish journalist.

Lazenby felt sweat breaking out on his body as he recalled Gosta's matter-of-fact offer to sleep with him. She was a clever, resourceful woman, who might easily have reasoned that posing as Lazenby's mistress could provide a credible alternative explanation for her presence in his car. Had he been foolish and reckless enough to agree to demean himself by such a "bargain" she would no doubt have managed to book herself a room in the hotel. She would naturally have dined with him, and later "discreetly" come to his room, in the certain knowledge that such an assignation would become known to the security police. It was no secret that they generally bugged hotel rooms used by foreigners, and Gosta might calculate that if she played her part convincingly they would be likely to conclude that her motive in joining Lazenby was simply to enjoy a spot of furtive nooky.

Where *was* Gosta now, anyway? Was she still lurking on the premises, hoping to enact such a scenario even now? Or had she secreted the tape somewhere in his car in spite of her earnest assurance to the contrary? Lazenby went over to the hand basin and splashed tepid water over his face, hoping it would help to clear his weary mind. Then, leaving his briefcase on the bed, he went downstairs to the lobby. If anybody wanted to read the copy of Julian Symons's *Bloody Murder* he'd abstracted from the British Council library in Budapest, or a boring British Council file, or study the raw material of his next travel and subsistence claim while he was out of the room, they were welcome.

The male receptionist who had checked him in about twenty minutes earlier was still behind the desk. He spoke much less eccentric English than Enescu, though his Groucho Marx moustache made Lazenby half expect rapid-fire wisecracks rather than the melancholy courtesy with which he answered Lazenby's questions. After a brief conversation about meal arrangements, Lazenby asked with careful nonchalance about the foreign lady who had come in to ask about train times.

Ah, yes, the man explained, the lady had been fortunate indeed in her timing. An international express train from Bucharest to Vienna via Budapest was due to depart from Arad at a few minutes after six, and she had left the hotel by taxi for the twenty-minute drive to the station well before four. The lady had mentioned that her Romanian exit/re-entry permit was in order, that she had a valid visa for Hungary and was in a position to pay for a ticket in hard currency. Most certainly, therefore, she would be able to buy one at the ticket office and to clear customs and immigration at Arad Station, the control point on the Romanian side of the border, in good time to board the train. It was due to reach Budapest at about eleven in the evening. Lazenby was so relieved to learn that Gosta was on her way, having probably been doing nothing more remarkable than making use of the hotel's ladies' room while he was checking in, that he made up his mind there and then to stretch his legs before the sun finally disappeared and it turned chilly.

Once outside, he stood for a moment, hands in pockets in a proprietorial stance, in front of the entrance. It was still quite mild, but the fresh, pine-scented air of the Transylvanian Alps was already a distant memory. When Lazenby sniffed, his nose registered a stale dustiness laced with acrid fumes from the exhausts of passing vehicles.

Big trucks, like the two parked Bulgarian lorries whose compressors were growling away at the side of the car park, belched out black diesel smoke, while rattletrap pick-ups and the few cars – mostly East German Trabants – were running on the same foul-smelling low-octane petrol whose reek pervaded the polluted air of downtown Budapest.

The landscape was as flat and featureless as the Hungarian *puszta*, which was only to be expected: Arad was in fact situated at the eastern end of the same great plain and the frontier was not many miles to the west. With the trucks under police guard, Lazenby saw no harm in leaving the environs of the hotel for an hour or so, and he decided to stroll in the direction of the town. If it was as near as he thought, he might as well explore it briefly before going back to the hotel for a pre-dinner drink and a dip into *Bloody Murder* to take his mind off Gosta and her confounded cassette tape.

As soon as he rounded the first bend he could see a scatter of buildings ahead, and passed a signpost bearing an arrow and the word CENTRUM. He walked as far as what seemed to be the town's central square but then turned back: such fleshpots as Arad apparently offered lacked obvious appeal, and the shop window displays were markedly more drab than those to be seen in Hungarian provincial towns of comparable size. To his own mild suprise Lazenby found himself looking forward to being back in Budapest, which boasted in and around fashionable Vaci Utca a number of expensive boutiques and elegant restaurants. It would be good to sit and drink coffee at a table outside the Victorian grandeur of the Vorosmarty or Red Star Café, so named when it was taken over by the state in 1948 but still obstinately referred to by all Budapest residents as Gerbaud's after its famous French founder-proprietor. Some of the diplomatic community wittily called it the Very Smarty Café, but the joke was lost on most Hungarians.

Lazenby was wearing an elderly but good quality tweed sports jacket with a roll neck sweater, a pair of Daks flannels and comfortable shoes, and felt sure that his clothes and general comportment marked him out as a westerner. There were plenty of pedestrians about, and it occurred to him as he retraced his steps that he hadn't made eye contact with a soul. The people who passed him not only paid him no attention, but were inclined to look away. It was as though they were avoiding the evil eye, he thought: then he stopped short in amazement. He had caught a glimpse of two children rounding a corner about a hundred metres ahead of him, a small boy and a slightly bigger girl, and though he had seen them for a mere fraction of a second, they looked uncommonly like Agnes and Sandor.

He felt goose pimples rise on his forearms and back. Surely not! It just *couldn't* be, not again, not here in Arad. Lazenby hesitated, and then walked to the corner as fast as he could without breaking into a run. By the time he got there, no children were to be seen, and after dabbing the sweat from his forehead with a paper handkerchief he continued on his way back to the hotel, more than a little shaken and trying to convince himself that a combination of weariness, anxiety and continuing remorse about Gosta was making him conjure gipsy children out of his imagination. Of one thing he was quite sure: he needed a drink.

"So where is he now?" The hotel receptionist had never to his knowledge set eyes on the owner of the gravelly voice at the other end of the line, but spoke to him in the line of duty more often than he would have liked.

"He left the hotel on foot a few minutes ago, heading towards town. The woman ordered a taxi to take her to the station well before then. I suppose he could be making his way there too, but I can't think why."

"Leave the thinking to us, comrade. Let me know what time he gets back, and meantime have a quick look through his luggage. We'll check his car later." The receptionist sighed as he put the phone down, and patted his pocket to make sure that he had his pass key. He was an ethnic Hungarian, and it was distasteful to him to have to act as a low-grade spy for the security police. On the plus side, it was now possible to telephone to Budapest by dialling direct, and he planned to do so shortly. He had relatives in that city, and one of his kinsmen was always pleased to receive any interesting information about visiting diplomats.

Chapter Ten

Brooding thoughts about the gipsy children and pangs of self-loathing over his cowardly refusal to help Gosta dominated Lazenby's consciousness throughout the evening and led to a troubled night's sleep, and still nagged at him next morning while he showered, dressed and packed his case. They were displaced only towards the end of his breakfast, by the appearance of the dapper Lieutenant Enescu. He came into the dining room full of the joys of spring, marched over to Lazenby's table and saluted snappily, beaming at him. It was a little after seven-thirty.

"*Bonjour*! Enescu is early," he announced. "*Vous avez bien dormi?*" Without waiting for Lazenby to reply, Enescu pointed dramatically at his plate, on which were the remains of his breakfast. This had consisted of two doorstep slices of bread, a huge sausage which had been brought still steaming on a plate alongside a liberal helping of German-style mustard, a small pot of muddy "coffee" and some of the ubiquitous bright red jam.

"You like our famous Romanian *saucisson*." It was a statement, not a question. When the Hungarian-speaking waitress first placed the monstrosity before him Lazenby had contemplated it with foreboding, but after a while it occurred to him that it was nothing more than an oversized Hungarian *krinolin* and he attacked it with a good appetite and disposed of over two-thirds.

"Good morning, Lieutenant. I'm almost ready." Lazenby

decided neither to comment on the quality of his night's rest nor to embark on a discussion of the sausage. "Will you sit down and have a cup of coffee? I could order some more for you."

"*Non, merci.* Enescu drinks not on the duty."

Lazenby shrugged. "As you wish. I'll settle my account, and then join you outside, shall I?" Standing, he drained the last of his coffee, which was a mistake since it left him with an evil-tasting sludge in his mouth, and trailed in Enescu's wake out of the dining room. The Lieutenant strode over to the cashier's desk and rapped on it imperiously, but Lazenby ignored him and went up to his room to clean his teeth. When he returned again to the lobby with his suitcase and briefcase his bill was ready for him but Enescu had disappeared.

As soon as Lazenby stepped outside the entrance he saw his minder again. He wasn't far away. With a less elegantly turned out colleague he was striding briskly about ten metres in one direction and then turning about to retrace his steps, putting Lazenby in mind of a Guards Officer waiting to go on parade. Lazenby went straight to his car, put the suitcase in the boot and his briefcase on the front passenger seat, and only then walked over to intercept the two policemen half way along the leg of the course they were following.

"Ready when you are, Lieutenant. Oh good, the truck drivers are present and correct, I see." The Bulgarians were standing beside one of the vehicles with cigarettes dangling from their mouths and looking just as depressed as they had on the previous day. Lazenby was tempted to go over and ask them if they'd had a good time during their evening off, but didn't feel that his German was up to it. So he gave them a friendly wave and a smile instead, and was rather hurt when they turned their backs on him.

"Okay," Enescu said. "We go. Gasoline station first.

You follow Enescu, *n'est ce pas?*" Pursued by his colleague, he moved quickly over to one of two police cars, shouting something at the Bulgarians and making a large beckoning arm movement which made him look for all the world like John Wayne leading a company of US Cavalry. They seemed to understand, and clambered up into their cabs. A few seconds later black smoke belched from the diesel exhausts and they were on the move, with what Enescu had referred to the previous afternoon as the backside car, also with two uniformed men aboard, bringing up the rear.

The filling station was quite large, and did indeed sell premium grade petrol. After Lazenby had seen to the requirements of the Rover he had time, while diesel fuel was being pumped into the tanks of the lorries, to carry out a cursory search of his car. The glove compartment contained its usual jumble of crumpled peppermint packets and stubs of pencil as well as the owner's manual and a tattered giveaway map of western European autoroutes, but no cassette tape. A quick feel around the underside of the dashboard was equally reassuring. Gosta might just have made an opportunity to attach it there, but she had at no time been alone in the car and he would surely have noticed if she had secreted it anywhere else in the interior.

With much comradely shouting and confident gestures and winks on the part of Lieutenant Enescu, the convoy got under way again. Lazenby was impressed anew by the amount of manpower the Romanians had deployed in order to ease their passage. As on the previous day, there were policemen on point duty to wave them over major crossings and stand to attention as Lazenby passed, and they were soon clear of Arad. The officials at the border checkpoint at Nadlac had been alerted, and they barely troubled to look at the Bulgarian drivers' papers. Lazenby found it hard to believe that Boris and

Ivan normally enjoyed such treatment at East European frontiers.

Nor did the customs man linger over the documents which Dalby had handed to Lazenby in Bucharest and which specified in detail the contents of the packing cases in the lorries. They bore the official impress of the Museums Directorate of the Romanian Ministry of Culture, which seemed to have a magical effect.

His passport duly stamped and returned to him, Lazenby went over to make his farewells to Enescu and his men in a markedly more cheerful mood than he had been in when he had woken up. The officials speeding him on his way had not behaved like men on the alert for a possible attempt to smuggle out under diplomatic cover material which would if published be deeply embarrassing to their political masters. Nor had there been yet another real or imagined sighting of Agnes and her brother Sandor that morning.

After accepting with becoming gravity a formal salute from all four members of his police escort, Lazenby seized Enescu's hand and shook it warmly. He felt that a short official speech was called for, and cleared his throat portentously.

"Well, thank you again, Lieutenant Enescu. The journey from Bucharest has been most pleasant, and has been accomplished more smoothly than I would have thought possible, thanks to the splendid co-operation extended to me by you, your police colleagues, and of course the museum and other authorities in Bucharest. On behalf of Her Majesty's government I should like, in taking my leave, to pay tribute to your efficiency and courtesy, and express my heartfelt personal thanks to you all."

Lieutenant Enescu nodded with a hint of impatience throughout what Lazenby himself judged to be a pretty nauseating performance, and pausing only as if to confirm that no more diplomatic clichés were to follow, clicked his heels and bowed curtly.

"*Bien, bien*, is enough, yes? Now you go. Enescu says *bon voyage*. Okay? Be seeing you."

Startled by this sudden burst of plain speaking, Lazenby reverted to his native vernacular. "Right, cheers then," he said, resisting the temptation to add the word "squire". While opening the door of the Rover, he managed to catch the eye of Boris, perched high in his cab, and indicated with gestures that they were off. The striped barrier across the road was raised, more salutes all round, and then all three vehicles were traversing the corridor of two hundred metres or so of no man's land between Romania and Hungary.

Lazenby was now feeling distinctly chirpy. It was good to have Romania behind him, and to be able to look forward to annoying Viktor Szekacs by enthusing about the Romanians. They really had done well, even handsomely, by him. The effervescent Lieutenant Enescu might be a touch eccentric, but he wasn't in the same league as Dracula's unpredictable Comrade Nagy.

Another warming thought occurred to him. In spite of the fact that she must have been disappointed by his unco-operativeness, Gosta Lundin had in making her farewells expressed a willingness to renew and further their acquaintance in Budapest, barely four hours' drive away now. She hadn't said where she would be staying, but he had several friendly Scandinavian contacts and it wouldn't be difficult to find out.

As he left Nadlac, Lazenby began to whistle tunelessly, and looked at the dashboard clock. It was just coming up to nine forty-seven, and he was in sight of the Hungarian barrier and customs post on the other side. According to his map it was called Nagylak. Nagylak/Nadlac: obviously the officials of the two countries glared at each other in fraternal socialist hostility from opposite ends of the same village.

As he began to slow down, a uniformed official emerged

from the cluster of small buildings with the Hungarian flag fluttering above them. Ten o'clock, he'd agreed with Dracula, and he was five minutes early. Not bad, not bad at all.

Chapter Eleven

At the age of thirty-one, Lajos Ranki was, all his colleagues agreed, far too mild and agreeable a man to be suited to the job of Customs Inspector. Some years in the occupation had taught him to be on the lookout for most of the pathetically obvious tricks employed by amateur smugglers, however, and he usually caught such people out. When he did, he rarely threw the book at offenders among Hungarians returning from the West, preferring to confiscate their illicit hard currency, cigarettes, coffee or copies of Playboy. Then he would admonish them in terms of such gentle reproach that he often brought tears of remorse to their eyes. Ranki genuinely didn't like getting people into trouble, and besides, his wife Kati liked the little treats he brought home or was able to afford to buy for her.

Until recently, his had been on the whole an agreeable way of life, though it pained him that he had to pretend to be unaware of Kati's waywardness. She was a sensual woman who effortlessly attracted male attention, and being childless and employed as an assistant in a barber shop, was in a position to enjoy it to the full, particularly when Lajos was on night duty.

However, both Kati and her husband had faced a serious disruption of their routines when a few weeks earlier Lajos had been transferred from a post on the border with Austria to one on the opposite side of the country. The traffic from Romania yielded appallingly meagre pickings; and after a few tense weeks in their cramped new quarters in nearby Szeged, Kati had packed her plastic suitcase and taken herself off to seek fulfilment in Budapest. Worse, Lajos had the previous day received a curt letter from her, advising him that she had filed for divorce. Not surprisingly in the circumstances, he was in a thoroughly bloody-minded mood.

The flighty Kati's departure from her husband's side was the main reason why, two hours after the meat transporters and the Rover crossed into Hungarian territory, Lazenby and the landscape paintings were not bowling along half way to Budapest as he had confidently expected to be before lunchtime. The three vehicles had in fact progressed no more than a hundred and fifty metres or so, and were parked in a lay-by beside the customs building.

Inside, sweating with frustration and embarrassment over the inadequacies of his command of the Hungarian language, Lazenby was on the telephone trying to find out where the hell Szekacs was, and why none of the officials at the Nagylak border post had been warned to expect and instructed to admit him and the consignment in his charge.

Ivan and Boris, no doubt conditioned by long experience to cope with unscheduled delays, had descended from their cabs and were outside, stretching themselves and rolling their shoulders in a slightly menacing manner. Lazenby knew nothing of Lajos Ranki's marital problems, of course, but had gathered that he seemed to be in charge and professed to be unable to speak or understand English. Ranki had nevertheless grudgingly permitted Lazenby to use the telephone, remaining at his desk throughout. He was, Lazenby inferred, deeply suspicious not only of the two Bulgarians, whose grimy passports he occasionally pushed about on the surface of his desk with a disdainful forefinger, but also of Lazenby's own *bona fides*.

This was apparent from the way he repeatedly leafed through the pages of his British passport while Lazenby struggled with the phone, scrutinising the cancelled diplomatic visa for the Romanian visit in particular with a contemptuous curl of the lip, before turning his attention yet again to the ID card issued by the Hungarian Ministry of Foreign Affairs. Ranki must in the exercise of his duties have seen similar documents many times before, but something about the way he handled it, gazing first at the photograph inside and then up at Lazenby's tormented features, suggested strongly to Lazenby that he regarded it as an unusually clumsy forgery.

Lazenby had already telephoned the British Embassy in Budapest and succeeded in getting through to Loo Brush, to whom he reported his predicament. The Head of Chancery was maddeningly laconic, and had nothing more encouraging to suggest than that the missing Viktor Szekacs would probably turn up sooner or later and sort things out. When asked very politely if he, Loo Brush, would himself be so good as to telephone the Institute of Cultural Relations just round the corner in Vorosmarty Square and persuade somebody there to intercede with the customs authorities, he flatly refused.

"My dear Ben," he had protested, the pain in his tone coming through clearly in spite of the fizzes and crackles on the line, "I have no more intention of doing your job for you than of asking you to do mine. Manifestly you have access to a telephone, and if I am not mistaken, you are paid an extra two hundred and forty pounds a year in recognition of your pass in Intermediate Standard Hungarian. I suggest you start earning it by dealing with the customs authorities and discovering the whereabouts of your Mr Szekacs for yourself."

Lazenby had taken and sailed through the Foreign Office language examination at Lower Standard before leaving London, and his achievement in passing at Intermediate Standard a few months after his arrival in Budapest was a sore point with the Head of Chancery, to whom had fallen the task of supervising Lazenby, the sole local candidate.

Lazenby's written translations from and into Hungarian were sent to London for marking, but the oral test prescribed at intermediate standard was conducted by the approved examiner, an elderly lecturer at Eotvos Lorand University in Budapest. Loo Brush had been present as the Embassy's observer at what Lazenby in his heart of hearts had to agree was a delightful farce.

The dear old boy was clearly determined from the outset to pass him, and amiably hogged the conversation, leaving Lazenby to say little more than good afternoon in Hungarian as he entered the room, yes or no as appropriate, and thank you very much when he was dismissed with an avuncular smile and requested to wait outside.

When Loo Brush emerged after his private discussion with the examiner his face was red and he could barely contain his fury. Grudgingly confiding to Lazenby that when filling in and signing the official result sheet the old man had insisted on awarding him ninety per cent for his performance, he had gone on to say that in his opinion such a mark was preposterous, that the test should be declared null and void, and that he would so recommend in his covering report to London.

Had he expressed himself a little more graciously and shown the slightest sense of humour about the matter, Lazenby might have been inclined to agree with him. As it was, he heard Loo Brush out in offended silence, and rejoiced when a few weeks later he was formally notified that he had passed the written papers comfortably and the oral test with a remarkable ninety per cent.

His small victory had been sweet, but now he was

definitely hoist with his own petard and faced with a real linguistic challenge. After getting two wrong numbers, probably because his fingers were so slippery with sweat that he had misdialled, he eventually found himself speaking to a person who admitted that he had reached the KKI, or Institute of Cultural Relations. Heedless of grammar or syntax, Lazenby managed to convey his urgent desire to be put through to somebody, anybody, in the department concerned with the Anglo-Hungarian Cultural Agreement.

Then he waited, mopping his face in relief, confident that whoever picked up the phone would understand English. He was mistaken. A male voice asked in Hungarian what he wanted. "May I speak English?" he said, smiling hopefully at the telephone.

"*Nem ertem. Beszel magyarul,*" came the curt reply, and at once Lazenby's confidence deserted him again. He couldn't remember whether or not he had on the day of the drive to Debrecen heard Comrade Nagy actually utter words, but in his misery the wild thought came to him that he was very possibly speaking to him now, and that Nagy having somehow learned of his disparaging remarks about him was taking his revenge.

He did his best to formulate in halting Hungarian the simple request to speak to somebody in English, but knew he was making a hash of it, and switched to an incoherent mixture of English and German instead, babbling about the British Embassy, the Anglo-Hungarian Cultural Agreement and the exhibition which was due to be opened at the National Gallery in Heroes' Square a few days hence and was covered by officially certified documentation but was being held up in spite of that by an unhelpful official at the customs post at Nagylak.

The man at the other end of the line must have decided that he was dealing with a lunatic, because after Lazenby stuttered himself to a standstill a very brief silence ensued, followed by the sound of a receiver being replaced.

Lazenby clutched the phone in frustration and despair, and realised just in time that he was in serious danger of actually weeping. Pulling himself together, he hung on for a few seconds, from time to time nodding vigorously and grunting as if in agreement. "Excellent. Thank you. I knew you would understand. I will pass that on to the responsible official here," he then said in English to the dialling tone, and put the phone down with such dignity as he could muster.

Filled with indignation, Lazenby found that he had miraculously recovered his command of Hungarian, and he addressed Lajos Ranki in that language, stiffly but reasonably correctly. First he thanked him for the use of his telephone, then told him he had spoken to senior officials at both the British Embassy and the KKI. That the deputy to the British Ambassador had expressed concern, and the representative of the Institute of Cultural Relations sincere regret over the delayed arrival of Mr Szekacs. The KKI official had agreed that it was imperative that the paintings should arrive in Budapest before evening, and suggested that the convoy should set out at once, undertaking that the vehicles would be intercepted approximately half way, at or near the town of Kecskemet, by a KKI car and escorted the rest of the way into the capital.

Lazenby found himself warming to his own inventive eloquence, but was as surprised as he was gratified when his lies produced the required effect. The customs man sat through the performance in silence, but then grunted and reached for the exhibition documentation Lazenby had placed before him. After peering at the papers once more he shrugged and seemingly decided to throw in the towel. He picked up an impressive-looking official stamp, pressed it to an ink-pad and then, after a final hesitation that seemed to last for hours, rapidly endorsed all three passports and the consignment note, and pushed everything across the desk to Lazenby.

After watching the Englishman leave the customs office and walk over to the three vehicles, Lajos Ranki took out his handkerchief, and picked up the telephone. Having fastidiously wiped Lazenby's sticky fingermarks from the receiver, he then rang the Szeged police headquarters and told the duty officer there that a man claiming to be a British diplomat was about to pass through the outlying town of Maros, allegedly bound for Budapest and escorting two large lorries with Bulgarian drivers. "And there's another thing . . ." Ranki said, and lowered his voice.

Major Grigory Vishinski of the Soviet Army listened to the lieutenant who acted as his liaison officer with the Hungarian police with some interest. As officer commanding a vehicle maintenance and repair depot, his was, he was all too aware, a dead end job, and he welcomed any diversion.

"You say this man was only pretending to talk to the KKI in Budapest?"

"Yes, Comrade Major. The customs officer could hear the dialling tone most of the time."

Vishinski reached for a piece of scrap paper and a pencil. "What did he say his name was?" He listened and scribbled L-Y-N-Z-B-Y. Vishinski was proud of his mastery of the roman alphabet. "Got it. Leave it with me."

The one personal advantage the Major enjoyed in his dreary posting with the Soviet forces garrisoned in Hungary was that his cousin Pavel was the Assistant Military Attaché at the Soviet Embassy in Budapest, and he decided to tell him about this curious incident. One never knew, if there was anything in it Pavel might out of gratitude be persuaded to pull strings and arrange for him to be reassigned to somewhere a bit less off the beaten track.

Light-headed after his ordeal at the customs post, Lazenby had the briefest of conferences in fractured German with Boris and Ivan. He managed, he believed, to make them understand that they were to follow his car, keep in sight of each other and of him, and stop only when he did unless in an emergency, in which case they were to flash their headlights. Then he set off at a cracking pace before Lajos Ranki changed his mind.

They negotiated the bustling city of Szeged in fine style without benefit of policemen on point duty, and drove along the highway as it veered north-west across the great plain towards unpronounceable Kiskunfelegyhaza and then Kecskemet, the last substantial town before Budapest itself. After they had rumbled through Kiskunfelegyhaza, a railway junction town with a fine display of venerable, snorting steam locomotives, Lazenby noticed a roadside tavern with wooden tables and benches outside, and judged it safe to pause there for refreshments.

Having triumphed over the obstructive customs man and demonstrated to his own satisfaction that he could do without the likes of the Draculas and Loo Brushes of this world, Lazenby was in an expansive mood. It was just coming up to half-past one, and at the rate they were travelling they would be at their destination by well before four even after a short break. He signalled his intention to pull to the side of the road, and saw in his rear-view mirror that the driver immediately behind him had got the message.

Safely parked, he got out of the car and stretched while he waited for the truck drivers to follow suit. When they climbed down he grinned at them and raised an imaginary glass to his lips, and in response they went so far as to crack a glum smile. A beer apiece wouldn't hurt any of them, he decided, even though the permitted level of alcohol for drivers in the People's Republic of Hungary was nil. So he stood a round of drinks and the inevitable rolls with hot sausages and mustard, and what passed for general goodwill prevailed.

After about twenty minutes Lazenby looked meaningfully at his watch and paid the bill. Ivan made for the ramshackle urinal beside the tavern, and when he emerged, Boris followed his example. Lazenby went last, making his visit as short as possible. He had no reason to imagine that the drivers would make off without him, but he wasn't inclined to risk it. Besides, the facilities were very primitive, and malodorous in the extreme.

By five minutes to two they were moving again, on the last lap, and Lazenby was feeling good. Only Kecskemet and a few small villages now lay between the convoy and Budapest. God alone knew what Viktor Szekacs thought he was doing, but Lazenby knew the way to the National Fine Art Gallery and had met the Senior Curator responsible for arranging the display of the paintings. All would be well once they arrived. The drivers would presumably go on their mysterious way as soon as the crates had been unloaded, checked off against his list and taken into the Gallery premises. Finally, having thankfully handed over responsibility to the Gallery authorities, he would be able to go to his palatial house, have a much-needed bath and savour a very large, well-earned whisky.

Lazenby was still so much absorbed in his pleasing reverie that on the approach to Kecskemet he failed to notice the road sign warning drivers that there was a low bridge ahead. Nor did the arrow indicating an alternative route for heavy goods vehicles requiring more than 2.5 metres of clearance register on his consciousness. He drove on, followed by the first of the two lorries.

Chapter Twelve

In the circumstances, the local traffic police officer was very reasonable when he arrived from Kecskemet on his bicycle to inspect the damage inflicted on the bridge by the rogue Bulgarian meat transporter which was firmly wedged beneath it. So was his superior, who came in a car, having been summoned when the patrolman realised after looking at Lazenby's ID card that he had a distressed British diplomat on his hands as well as a belligerent Bulgarian driver.

Having in his turn studied the diplomatic identity card, the new arrival handed it back to Lazenby, sized up the situation and took charge with commendable resourcefulness and speed, turning his attention first to Boris. Boris was shouting in what had to be his own language, and gesticulating wildly, occasionally pausing to point contemptuously at Lazenby. Lazenby couldn't understand a word, but the man's meaning was clear: he was telling the world at the top of his voice that it wasn't his fault, but that of the incompetent bloody idiot of an Englishman, who had done nothing but balls everything up since they had left Bucharest.

The senior man soon shut him up, by shouting even more loudly at him, in what Lazenby was able to recognise as Russian, with miraculous effect. Boris simmered down at once and shuffled uneasily, avoiding eye contact as the policeman continued in Russian, at reduced volume, pointing at the tyres of the lorry, which the driver and the other policeman promptly set to work to deflate. By this simple expedient the lorry was soon dislodged. It was then possible for it to be backed out and parked by the side of the road, and for Lazenby to bring his own car back from the far side of the bridge and face the music.

While his subordinate waved the considerable line of interested drivers of waiting vehicles on their way, the resourceful officer introduced himself as Sergeant Miklos Hunyadi. He was a huge bear of a man with a splendid soup-strainer moustache and sad brown eyes, who looked about fifty and proved to have a better command of English than Lazenby had of Hungarian. This was just as well, since Lazenby made the alarming deduction in the absence of any sign of him that Ivan, bringing up the rear, must have obeyed the diversion sign and taken the alternative route. The mental image of the second lorry careering away across the great Hungarian plain, unescorted and with half a million pounds worth of paintings on board reduced their temporary custodian to a gibbering wreck.

The estimable Sergeant Hunyadi refused to be flustered, and revealed a completely different side to his character from that displayed in his brusque dealings with the Bulgarian. He was sympathetic, even affectionate, wrapping a beefy arm round Lazenby's trembling shoulders, listening to him with a kindly smile, and speaking in a soothing rumble. He smelt strongly of sweat and garlic, but Lazenby found comfort in his embrace, and gradually calmed down. He realised that Hunyadi was unlikely to have grasped the finer points of his explanation of what a British diplomat was doing in charge of a Bulgarian and a very large lorry on the outskirts of Kecskemet, but his new protector did seem to understand that there was every reason to believe that another vehicle had gone its own way and that this was a matter of pressing concern to him. Releasing Lazenby from his encircling arm, Hunyadi turned to Boris for confirmation, firing a few peremptory questions at him in Russian and nodding at the man's surly but prompt replies.

Finally the big man, attended by his colleague, walked with measured tread all the way round the lorry, inspecting it closely, before standing in the middle of the road a few paces from the bridge and scrutinising the brickwork of the arch. Apparently satisfied that such damage as had been caused by the impact was minor, and clearly enjoying his opportunity to influence the course of negotiations with possible international implications, Sergeant Hunyadi turned his attention once more to Lazenby, looking mournful but compassionate.

"You English man," he said, with a clear pause between the second and third words.

"Yes. I am a First Secretary at the British Embassy in Budapest," Lazenby said with heavy emphasis, pointing to the government crest on his card. Hunyadi made a dismissive gesture, as though unwilling to take account of such trifles. Then he put his vast face very close to Lazenby's and gazed soulfully into his eyes.

"You visit Ealing one time?"

"Ealing? In west London?"

"So. Ealing."

Taken aback, Lazenby nodded. Ealing wasn't the sort of place people actually visited, in his experience, but he knew roughly where it was and must surely have driven through it from Fulham from time to time on his way to somewhere else.

The sergeant grinned with pleasure, revealing an appalling collection of irregular and discoloured teeth. "You know my liddle sister," he stated with conviction and immense satisfaction. "Ilona. Missis Sturgess. Number Twelve Baldwin Street."

Lazenby didn't dare to deny it. Indeed he was quite ready if it seemed advisable to swear that he was a cordial acquaintance of Mrs Ilona Sturgess née Hunyadi – and of her husband, of course – and, as such, frequently dropped in at their Baldwin Street residence for a cup of tea and a chat. He must at all costs keep this imposing representative of the Kecskemet police force on his side. "Ilona Sturgess? Oh yes, I'm sure we've met. I don't like to rush you, Sergeant, but I'm very anxious to – "

"In fifty-six she *kislany*. Liddle girl. Go with mother to Becs, you call Wien. Then England. Me, I stay, fight Russian tanks," Hunyadi rumbled on inexorably. Looking at the granite set of his jaw, Lazenby could well believe that he had done just that, with improvised Molotov cocktails and his bare hands. All at once his own concerns seemed very trivial, and he felt ashamed.

"So your sister grew up in England and is now married and living in Ealing. You must miss her very much, Sergeant."

"Bloody right. She come back last year with Trevor for visit. Trevor bloody good bloke." Lazenby inferred that the Sergeant had not only enjoyed meeting his British brother-in-law but also learned some useful colloquialisms from him. He closed his eyes briefly and gave thanks for Trevor Sturgess, obviously a stout fellow and his powerful if unsuspecting ally in his hour of need, while Hunyadi produced a massive pocket watch from his tunic and studied it with a frown before his face cleared. He smiled encouragingly at Lazenby.

"Okay. No problem. We help you turn round, then follow me. I put you on Budapest road sure. Then I telephone ahead, have other truck stop, wait for you." He draped one massive arm over Lazenby's shoulders again and gave him an agonising squeeze while shaking the hand imprisoned against his impressive belly before releasing him. As soon as he had recovered his breath, Lazenby spoke with fervent sincerity.

"Sergeant Hunyadi, thank you very much. You're a bloody good bloke."

"So what do we know about this man Lazenby?" The KGB Resident at the Soviet Embassy was away on business in Vienna and was in any case far too grand a personage to interest himself in such a minor matter as the movements of a middle-ranking British envoy. His deputy was holding the fort, however, and had given strict instructions that she was to be informed of any and every unusual incident referred to the section from any part of Hungary.

"I have copies of three reports made on him by the AVH. The first was soon after his arrival at post six months ago, the second was drawn up after a month of close surveillance and the most recent after a further three months of sporadic observation. We get copies of all such reports, of course."

"Yes, yes, I know that," the Deputy Resident said with a hint of testiness. The Hungarian security service was so anxious to please that they rather overdid the supply of paper. "Just give me the gist."

"Immediately, Comrade. Benjamin Lazenby is thirty-nine years old, 184 centimetres in height and weighs about eighty kilos. Grey eyes – "

"The important thing is to establish whether or not he's an SIS operative." The Deputy Resident rifled through a file at the side of her desk. "I can't find his name on my list."

"The AVH don't think so. He hasn't made any of the usual contacts, and the KKI report that, while having a strange sense of humour, he takes his cultural duties seriously. He attends orchestral concerts frequently, and the theatre from time to time."

"How unlike our own Cultural Attaché!"

The deferential assistant sniggered sycophantically at this shaft of wit, then cleared his throat and continued.

"On his concert and theatre visits he is usually accompanied by one of a number of women acquaintances, and he has been photographed in sexual activities of a conventional nature at his house with two of them during the past six months, one British and one American."

"At the same time? That's hardly conventional even nowadays."

"No, one at a time, and I forgot to mention that in any case he was divorced last year. He's reported to be a moderate to heavy drinker, and has been to Vienna on short local leave twice since he arrived. Nothing else noted."

"And what about these Bulgarian vehicles?"

"An art exhibition sponsored by the British Embassy is to be displayed here in Budapest beginning in a few days. The vehicles are said to contain oil paintings transferred from a similar event held in Bucharest last month."

"Then why on earth is this . . . Major Vishinski, is it? Why is he getting excited about them?"

"Well, it seems that he heard that there had been some trouble at the Nagylak frontier post not far from Szeged and that the subject behaved suspiciously; so he arranged for the convoy to be kept under discreet observation. Lazenby was observed drinking on friendly terms with the Bulgarian drivers at a roadside inn, and a report has just come in that a minor road accident has been staged in Kecskemet. In the confusion one of the trucks has disappeared."

"Well, if he cares all that much, perhaps the Major should go and look for it," said the Deputy Resident tartly.

Once clear of Kecskemet and waved on his way by Mrs Sturgess's kindly brother, Lazenby drove recklessly fast in the hope of catching up with the other meat lorry sooner rather than later, checking in his rear-view mirror to make quite sure that Boris was keeping up with him. He was, and seemed to be enjoying himself, waving merrily as his juggernaut thundered along behind, relieved no doubt to have been released so unexpectedly from the clutches of the Hungarian police.

Lazenby hoped very much that Hunyadi would be as good as his word and arrange for the second truck to be stopped, but pressed on at high speed all the same. So much so that when he spied a black, official-looking car coming up from far behind with headlights blazing and horn sounding, his shoulders slumped as he took his foot off the accelerator and switched on his rear lights to warn the Bulgarian behind him that he was stopping. The lorry had pneumatic brakes, thank God. Lazenby was heartily fed up. After all he'd been through, it was particularly galling to be pulled up for speeding.

However, it wasn't a police car that snaked in ahead of the Rover and braked so abruptly that Lazenby was hard put to it to avoid colliding with its rear end. It was the Chaika belonging to the Institute of Cultural Relations, with a grinning Comrade Nagy at the wheel and a pale Viktor Szekacs in the passenger seat beside him.

Lazenby got out of his car, arranged his face in a grim and hostile expression and waited in silence as Szekacs approached. The situation put him in mind of the climactic confrontation in the main street of a frontier town in a bad Western movie, and in his righteous indignation he was sure which of them might be thought to be wearing the black hat and which the white. Lazenby half expected to see Dracula's hand hovering over a holster on his hip. He decided to beat him to the draw by using his favourite psychological tactic in such situations.

It had been recommended to him during his first overseas posting years before, when he was about to return to Britain on his first long home leave. Bob Smithers, an old lag of a colleague who neither desired nor merited promotion, drew him on one side and urged him, when reporting to his headquarters desk officer for debriefing, to say nothing whatsoever in response to conventional words of greeting. "Let the silence drag on, Ben. The other chap will crack if you stick it out, and then begin to blurt out apologies to you. Accept them grudgingly, and you'll be in the driver's seat for the rest of the interview."

Lazenby had been too young and green to follow this sage advice at the first opportunity, but bore it in mind and had employed the stratagem to excellent effect on a number of subsequent occasions over the years. He now stared in stony silence at Szekacs and watched his reactions of puzzlement followed by embarrassment. Sure enough, the KKI man broke first.

"Well, Mr Lazenby," he said. "I suppose I should apologise for my late arrival."

"Yes."

"I, ah, knew you were planning to return by way of Arad and the Nagylak border crossing."

"Yes. And you undertook to meet me there at about ten o'clock, Mr Szekacs. I was there on time. Why weren't you?"

Being addressed as Mr Szekacs rather than Viktor seemed to affect Dracula deeply. His shoulders sagged, and his expression changed to one of profound misery. "Comrade Nagy was convinced that you would return by the same route as that by which you left Hungary, namely by way of Oradea. It was his responsibility to telephone the officials at the appropriate border post and warn them to expect you, but he took it upon himself to alert those at the more northerly crossing at Artand instead. He insisted on driving us there rather than to Nagylak. I finally persuaded the officials at Artand that a mistake had been made, and requested Comrade Nagy to proceed to Nagylak with all speed. There is no direct route, and by the time we eventually arrived there you had set out."

Lazenby shook his head wearily and glanced over at the author of all his misfortunes that day. He was aware that Hungary's communist bureaucracy was provided with many nooks and crannies occupied by persons who were not what they appeared to be, and it had occurred to him already that in spite of his comparatively lowly status as a driver Comrade Nagy might be more important in the scheme of things than Dracula. Certainly he didn't look like a man who was nervous about his job security or career prospects, for he acknowledged Lazenby's interest him by nodding and raising a hand in what could be read as an affable gesture.

Turning back to Szekacs, Lazenby scowled at him. "And when you realised what was happening it didn't occur to you to ring the people at Nagylak and tell them about me? I was stuck there for two bloody hours, man! Or advise your own headquarters? I contacted the KKI myself, and got some complete idiot on the line for my pains."

While enjoying giving vent to his indignation, Lazenby realised that time was passing and there were more constructive things to be done. "I'll want to talk about this whole mess in detail later, Viktor, but for the moment we've got to catch up with the other lorry and press on to Budapest. I'll go in front, and you bring up the rear." Without waiting for a reply he strode over to his car, waved to Boris to follow, started the engine and roared off.

By the time they reached the outskirts of Budapest it was after four-thirty, and Lazenby's heart was once more in his boots, for there had been no sign on the way of the stray lorry. Glumly he drove on to the art gallery, hoping against hope to find it parked outside the staff and goods entrance.

It wasn't.

Chapter Thirteen

Lazenby finally drew up outside his house on the Buda side of the Danube just before eight and switched off the ignition. It was raining, and the few lights in the quiet street of dignified old houses made the surface of the road glisten. Instead of getting out of the car at once he continued to sit at the wheel with his head bowed, feeling very alone and sick to his stomach with anxiety.

The staff at the National Fine Art Gallery which occupied one side of Heroes' Square had been as helpful as it was reasonable for him to expect, given that it was nearly closing time and he had arrived not only several hours late, but with only half the promised material for the exhibition. Exhausted, Lazenby had left it to Szekacs to offer whatever explanation he could devise.

Whatever story Dracula cooked up seemed to mollify them. They arranged swiftly for the unloading of the packing cases from Boris's lorry and their transfer by trolley to the interior of the building. There, after checking that the official Romanian customs seals on them were unbroken, the Senior Curator formally accepted custody of the works of art described on the labels, by signing the list Lazenby produced from his briefcase. This was something of an act of faith on the Curator's part, because the cases would not be opened until the following day.

While Lazenby was watching the transfer of the cases, he noticed that Comrade Nagy had once more deserted his post and wandered towards the middle of the square, which is dominated by a huge monument. This consists of a plinth surmounted by a sculptural set piece depicting in heroic attitudes a number of the Magyar notables whose exploits are recorded in Hungarian school history textbooks. From a distance Nagy appeared to be studying the figures while smoking a cigarette, and something about his posture struck Lazenby even in his despondency as suggesting that the mysterious "chauffeur" confidently expected to be commemorated in stone himself in the fullness of time.

Meantime Boris was in a half-hearted way assisting with the unloading. He was whistling cheerfully, seemingly untroubled by the disappearance of his colleague and the other lorry, and it occurred to Lazenby for the first time that he too might be other than he purported to be. Were he and Nagy both in fact secret policemen? Did the Bulgarian's plans for the evening include a discreet visit to his Embassy for debriefing?

Meditating on the man's abrupt change of mood when, after shouting at him, the good Sergeant Hunyadi had – inexplicably no doubt to the Bulgarian – let him off without so much as a caution, Lazenby decided that such a thing was by no means impossible. At all events, by any commonsense reckoning it would be best for Boris's health to keep quiet about his brush with the Hungarian law.

Such speculation reminded Lazenby that he needed to shore up his own position vis-a-vis the Institute for Cultural Relations, and he drew on both his native low cunning and the survival techniques he had learned in the British Council's bureaucratic jungle to formulate a fall-back plan for the worst-case scenario: namely that the other driver had well and truly lost his way and that an official police search for him would have to be set in motion.

He could hardly imagine that the driver had, seeing an unexpected opportunity, hijacked the cargo in his lorry.

A couple of dozen oil paintings of the British landscape were hardly negotiable currency, and the enormous meat truck was highly conspicuous as well as in itself a valuable item whose loss would soon lead to questions being asked. Hungary was a small country, after all, with closely guarded borders. If the police authorities were to launch a full-scale search they would inevitably locate the missing vehicle and have it brought to Budapest, but such an exercise would generate a great fuss that would deeply embarrass the British Ambassador and result in hell to pay for Lazenby.

It had come on to rain as he headed purposefully towards the person he had decided to cast in the role of fall guy. Viktor Szekacs was clearly a shaken man, and his mental processes were sluggish. Lazenby even had to tug at his sleeve to induce him to move out of the rain. He gazed slack-jawed as Lazenby went on the offensive, insisting that Szekacs was must assume responsibility for finding the missing vehicle. Knowing as he spoke that his argument was specious and dishonest made Lazenby all the more eloquent.

He did not explain exactly how the two lorries had become separated, reasoning that the anglophile Sergeant Miklos Hunyadi of the Kecskemet police was in the highest degree unlikely to have reported the incident at the bridge to his superiors. Moreover, he would ensure that his underling kept quiet about it. There was no doubt that Hunyadi had stuck his neck out for Lazenby, but paradoxically he could be thanked most effectively by Lazenby's own silence.

Lazenby had studied the map with care, and knew that there was no major road junction between Kecskemet, where he had mislaid the lorry, and the suburbs of Budapest. The most likely explanation was that the second driver had found himself on the outskirts of the capital, and pulled off the road to wait for his colleague and

Lazenby to catch him up. Somehow in their agitation they must in fact have passed him, and the wretched man was still languishing somewhere quite near, possibly in a filling station with a parking area they might have overlooked.

Lazenby explained this theory to Szekacs, and told him firmly that he must go in the Chaika – or send Comrade Nagy on his own – and retrace the route as far as the point where they had finally made their belated rendezvous, checking carefully each and every possible stopping place for the missing vehicle. As a Hungarian official speaking his own language, he could make much more effective enquiries than an exhausted foreigner in a car with a number plate that tended to make ordinary citizens nervous. Then he delivered his knock-out punch.

"The only alternative I can think of, Viktor, is for me to make an official request through my Embassy for police assistance. I would regret having to do this, because in doing so I could scarcely avoid commenting on the contrast between the exemplary arrangements made by the Romanian authorities on their side of the frontier and the lamentable performance of the KKI in failing to honour your undertaking to meet us at Nagylak and escort us from there to Budapest."

It was a shabby threat, but it worked. After a pathetic attempt to pick holes in Lazenby's logic, Szekacs finally agreed to go in search of the lorry and take such other discreet action as proved necessary to track it down. Lazenby then announced that after dealing with the remaining paperwork at the museum, he would go straight to his house and remain there until he heard from Szekacs by phone. Then he watched with grim satisfaction as, with a hunted look, Dracula plodded through the rain to join Comrade Nagy. After a short but seemingly angry discussion they both embarked once more in the Chaika and Nagy drove away at breakneck speed.

* * *

Lazenby must have remained there brooding in the Rover outside his house for several minutes, and might even have fallen asleep had his dismal reverie not been abruptly disturbed by a rapping at the window beside him. It was misted up, and he could only dimly discern what appeared to be a female face peering through the glass. For a moment he couldn't remember where he was, but then pulled himself together and wound the window down. To his great surprise it was his Embassy colleague Joanna Crockett who had been trying to attract his attention.

"Joanna! You startled me. I was just collecting my thoughts before I went in. I'm just back from Bucharest. For heaven's sake, you're getting soaked. Come inside the house, have a drink or something." Lazenby hastened to get out of the car, produced the massive key to his front door from his briefcase and opened up, switching on the light in the entry hall. Joanna hung back in the doorway, looking sheepish.

"I knew you were due back today, but I thought it would be earlier. Look, Ben, I'm sorry to do this to you, but I've brought Emma Jarvis with me. She's waiting in my car just along the road. She turned up at the Embassy just before close of play, asking to see you urgently, and I went down to talk to her. She wouldn't tell me what it's about. I tried to ring you here, but there was no answer, of course, so I took her to my place to freshen up after her journey, gave her a drink and then thought I'd bring her here and see if you were about. Obviously she's going to need a bed for the night. I'd offer to put her up, but you know how small my flat is, and you've got masses of room, so . . ."

"Yes, yes, of course she can stay here. Go and fetch her, Joanna, while I get my things out of the boot."

The irruption of Emma and the obligation to make her welcome diverted Lazenby's mind from his troubles for a while. She apologised profusely for descending on him

112

the moment he arrived home, but Joanna firmly assured her that she was by no means the first British lecturer to turn up in Budapest in quest of rest and recreation and that Ben Lazenby was known to run a good pub. Initially appalled by the necessity to switch on an affably sociable manner, he managed to say most of the right things, showed the two women to a guest bedroom – he had two – and produced sheets and towels, leaving them to make up a bed for Emma while he washed quickly, changed and brought the rest of the house to life and warmth.

Knowing that Emma had something on her mind that she would be unlikely to divulge in her presence, Joanna stayed only long enough to accept and deal with a small glass of Tokay before tactfully taking her leave. Lazenby went downstairs with her to see her out, and Joanna extended her hands with a shrug of renewed apology. "Sorry, Ben," she mouthed, but Lazenby's spirits had risen a little at the prospect of company, and he gallantly kissed her on the cheek, telling her there was no need to apologise.

When he returned to the upstairs living room Emma was sitting in one of the huge *fin de siècle* armchairs with her hands demurely clasped in her lap like a well-mannered little girl at a party. She even politely thanked him for allowing her to stay overnight.

"Pleasure, I assure you. Um, you must be starving. I know I am. I'm afraid it'll have to be an omelette or whatever I can find in the fridge if you don't mind, though. My daily's a jolly good cook but I'm sorry to say she only does lunches. There's a first-rate restaurant just round the corner, but the thing is, I'm expecting an important phone call. First of all I need a bit of a sit-down and a proper drink, though. Are you happy with the Tokay, or can I get you a gin and tonic or something? I'm having a large whisky myself."

Emma demurely accepted another glass of Tokay and

Lazenby poured himself a heroic whisky to which he added a very much smaller amount of water. "Well, cheers again."

"I had no idea you lived in such grand style," Emma said after an awkward little pause. "I must admit I'm . . . well, a bit intimidated."

"The house goes with the job", Lazenby explained. "I don't mind telling you that I was intimidated myself when I first saw it. It knocks spots off Chateau Lazenby in Fulham, I assure you. The awful thing is how quickly one begins to take it for granted. Anyway, you can see that I rattle around in here on my own like one pea in a pod. Glad to put people up when I have the chance – oh, good, there's the phone. Excuse me a minute."

The telephone was in the kitchen and he rushed to answer it, knocking a chair over in the process. "Yes, Lazenby here."

After the usual series of clicks as the Hungarian security service tape recorder cut in, a faint but familiar voice could be heard over the background noise, which was as of bacon being fried. "This is Szekacs speaking, Mr Lazenby. I can inform you that the matter we discussed earlier is, ah, in the process of being resolved."

"Ah. Splendid." So Dracula realised that he too must watch his words on the phone. "Good. Well, I'll look forward to hearing about it tomorrow morning." They were to meet at the Art Gallery at ten.

"Yes. You must be tired after your long drive today, and I have much to do myself. So I will wish you good night."

"Right. Good night, Viktor. My regards to Comrade Nagy."

Lazenby crossed his eyes and stuck his tongue out rudely as he replaced the receiver, a profound sense of relief suffusing his whole being. Then he waltzed back into the living room, humming a little tune to himself, and seizing his glass of whisky, drained it quickly. This made him cough and wheeze, and he covered his embarrassment by pumping his elbows up and down in imitation of a cockerel, as Jack Nicholson had done so memorably in the film *Easy Rider*.

"You look very cheerful," Emma said with a smile. Lazenby noted with interest that during his brief absence she had replenished her glass, and recalled that she had enjoyed her fair share of alcohol during their evening together in Debrecen. It seemed much more than four days ago.

"I *am* cheerful. It was the message I was waiting for, and what I was hoping to hear. And it means that we can go out for a proper dinner after all. I think we've both earned it, and the rain seems to have stopped."

He put a finger to his lips and waved the other hand vaguely in the direction of the impressive chandelier-style ceiling light. He had no idea what Dr Emma Jarvis wished to discuss with him, but if it had induced her to take the train all the way from Debrecen for an impromptu visit it was presumably in some degree confidential. It might indeed be that she had helped herself to the Tokay in order to fortify herself for what was to come. Emma looked at the chandelier and, round-eyed, nodded in comprehension.

As soon as they were outside the front door, he spoke quickly. "You obviously got the point, Emma. My house is almost certainly bugged, and it wouldn't be wise to talk about private matters in the restaurant, which is just a short walk from here. So you can either tell me anything you want to on the way, or we'll go for a stroll afterwards."

"Oh, it can wait," Emma said, a slight huskiness in her voice, and firmly tucked her arm under his. So they made their way directly to the small but excellent restaurant called the Pest-Buda, where Lazenby was something of a regular and could count on being found a table, especially as late as nine in the evening.

Chapter Fourteen

In 1982 the Pest-Buda was one of the small Budapest restaurants which were, on account of their size, the nearest thing to private enterprise establishments permitted by the regime. Its prices were regulated and therefore low, and it was presided over with courtly charm by an elderly gentleman who took great pride in its ambience and the quality of the food served to the dozen or so patrons who could be accommodated at one time.

In the evenings a pianist whose long hair and ascetic features gave him a passing resemblance to the Abbé Liszt provided discreet background music. His repertoire consisted largely of sentimental ballads, and for a small consideration he accepted requests. Lazenby had discovered the place soon after his arrival and, being addicted to the singing of Edith Piaf, asked the pianist if he knew *If you love me, really love me*. He did, and thereafter played it whenever he noticed Lazenby among the diners.

When Lazenby walked in with Emma, the pianist was sitting quietly in a corner drinking a glass of wine, and they were welcomed and settled at a table for two without musical accompaniment. Emma, who seemed to be in a mood of elation scarcely to be accounted for by two or perhaps three glasses of Tokay, agreed with alacrity when Lazenby suggested that they should begin with deep-fried mushroom heads in feathery-light batter with sauce tartare, and proceed to roast goose with red cabbage, both specialities of the house. She also smiled happily at Lazenby's choice of wine, with which he prudently ordered a bottle of mineral water.

Soon the Liszt lookalike returned to his post, and began to play what Lazenby had come to think of as My Tune, *pianissimo*. Emma cocked her head to one side, said "What a lovely change from gipsy violins" and began to hum the melody, regarding Lazenby over the rim of her glass.

"You're quite something, you know, Ben," she then murmured. "A real man of mystery," after which delphic remark she sang softly along with the pianist, ". . . let it happen, I don't care . . ."

Feeling uncomfortable, Lazenby grinned bashfully and shook his head. "No, no. You've got me wrong, I'm afraid. I'm a very boring bureaucrat."

Their *gomba fejek* arrived and provided Lazenby with a brief respite during which he wondered what on earth had got into Emma, who had previously struck him as being admirably composed and self-contained, except when he had presented her with the bottle of Squezy in Debrecen. Her eyes were glistening and she was looking at him in a way he could only think of as moonstruck.

"Tell me about yourself, Emma," he said. "What made you apply for the Debrecen job?"

She blinked and shook her head as though emerging from a slight daze. "The Debrecen job? Oh, various reasons. Life in England had its personal complications, but my motives in asking for this job were quite positive. I want to learn Hungarian really well, for a start. My thesis was about Jonathan Swift, and I've dreamed up this theory that when he was thinking about devising a language for his Lilliputians he might have come across a Magyar glossary. Take their word for 'best', for example, *legjobb*. Doesn't that look and sound Lilliputian to you?"

"What an interesting notion! Yes, I suppose it does, in a way." Without considering the possible consequences,

Lazenby intoned a little poem that had stuck in his mind: "'Mo Rog/Glonog/Quinba/Hlinn varr.'"

"I beg your pardon?"

"It's a poem in Lilliputian, in that lovely book *Mistress Masham's Repose*. T.H. White. It means 'Give us a kiss, please Miss, I like your nose.'"

Emma burst into delighted laughter. "That's quite the nicest poem I've heard in years! T.H. White, did you say?"

"Yes. If you're interested in the Lilliputian language I'm surprised you don't know the book. Poor old White was an alcoholic gay and not very happy, but a marvellous writer all the same."

Emma smiled inscrutably. "And *do* you like my nose? Because if you do I'll gladly give you a kiss."

They surveyed each other in silence for a few seconds, Lazenby embarrassed and Emma Jarvis with half-closed eyes. Then Lazenby cleared his throat, and ostentatiously polished off the last of his mushrooms, all too conscious that Emma's lips were twitching deliciously and that she was willing him to respond.

"I think you've got a very charming nose," he muttered awkwardly in the end. She had, at that, and the hint of magic that had touched their first real meeting, in the restaurant in Debrecen, was in the air again, making his pulse race. Emma was a very attractive young woman, with something of the quizzical, intelligently humorous look of the young Ginger Rogers about her, and with quite as good a figure.

"Why thank you, kind sir," she said with a gracious inclination of her head, and then, as if sensing that enough was enough, went on to talk interestingly about Jonathan Swift as their roast goose was brought to the table and disposed of with relish.

It was about ten when they left the restaurant, and as soon as they were outside, Emma seized Lazenby's arm and clung to it possessively. "Oh Ben, that was a terrific meal. Thank you. Now I simply must talk to you properly. I know I said I could wait, but when it came to it I could hardly stop myself coming out with it in there. Let's go for that walk."

The sky was now clear, with just a few rags of cloud moving in front of the three-quarters moon, and the air smelt freshly washed as Lazenby piloted her the few hundred yards to the great Matthew Church and the terraces of the Fishermen's Bastion. They offer a stunning outlook over the glittering black Danube, with the Chain Bridge to the right and the parliament buildings across the river immediately opposite the Bastion on the Pest side of the city.

"Okay. We can talk now. What's on your mind, Emma?"

"Well, you are, actually. I'd never have guessed you'd be involved in something like this."

"Like what, for heaven's sake? You're not making any sense. Why don't you begin at the beginning?"

"All right, I'll try. You remember when you came to see La Horvath at the University? And when we went down to the lobby with you to see you off? Well, Professor Horvath went back in, but I was watching when you went to your car, and I saw those two children come up and talk to you. You gave them some money. Then that creepy Szekacs man charged up like a raging bull and tried to shoo them away and I saw you arguing with him. I got the impression that the kids got the better of him anyway."

"They did, too! And good luck to them. They were gipsies, as I expect you've gathered."

"Yes. After you'd driven off with him I beckoned them over and gave them a few forints myself. They'd spotted the blue plates on your car and asked if you lived in Budapest, and were you a friend of mine."

"Go on."

"Well, I saw no harm in saying yes, and that you did live in Budapest, but that you were on your way to Romania that day."

"Thank the lord for that," Lazenby said fervently, and Emma blinked at him in surprise.

"I'm glad you're not upset with me, but whatever d'you mean?"

"Doesn't matter. It's just that you've just partly explained a mystery that's been baffling me for days." He paused, noticed her puzzled expression, then decided to explain. "Oh, there's no harm in your knowing, I suppose. Those self-same kids were lying in wait for me when I got to Cluj late that same afternoon. I couldn't imagine how on earth they knew I was going there, and I still can't figure out how they managed to arrive before me, or indeed at all. There must be ways over the frontier the gipsies know about and the border guards don't."

"Well, I know they've been in Romania, but not that bit. Wow, this is getting more exciting all the time."

Lazenby abruptly freed his arm, put both hands on her shoulders and unceremoniously spun her round to face him. "What the hell do you mean, you know they've been to Romania? You must have seen them again!"

Emma nodded meekly. "Yes, I have. Very early this morning, in fact. When I got up I spotted them hanging about outside the block of flats where I live."

"And?"

"Well, I got dressed quickly and went down to see what they wanted. Just as well I did, wasn't it?"

As Lazenby stared at her in the moonlight, speechless, Emma finally enlightened him. She explained that the children told her they'd made their way from Cluj to Bucharest, guessing correctly that he would go to the British Embassy in that city.

Having spotted and recognised his distinctive car in the parking compound, they'd seen him drive off with another man in a car with Romanian diplomatic plates. They made themselves scarce, resuming their vigil early on the following morning, when Lazenby had returned with the same man and transferred to his own car again. Trailing him and Dalby to the Art Gallery, they had watched the bustle of departure and, from a safe distance, seen a blonde woman join Lazenby in his car. When it and the two lorries with their police escort set off, they had put two and two together to make half a dozen, somehow or other spirited themselves to Arad and once again outmanoeuvred Lazenby.

"Incredible. So it really was them I glimpsed in Arad, then. I thought I was going off my head."

"Oh, yes, they saw you there. And they saw the blonde arrive at the railway station. They were planning to stow away on the train and get back over the frontier that way. Anyway, you know how cheeky they are, apparently they went up to her as bold as brass and asked her why she wasn't driving across with you."

"They did *what*?"

"Exactly what I said." A wary note was discernible in Emma's tone as she continued. "Your lady friend is both resourceful and quick-thinking. And fluent in Hungarian, according to them."

"It comes easily to Finnish speakers." For some reason Lazenby found himself on the defensive. "And she's not my lady friend, at least not in the sense you seem to be implying. I'd met her at a party for the first time the previous evening and she hitched a ride to Arad over my strong objections. Her name is Gosta Lundin and I'm told she's a well-known journalist."

"That's what she told the children, too. Anyway, she talked to them at some length as soon as she learned that they knew so much about you and why, and came to a quick decision. She gave them something to take into Hungary for her, and made them promise to get it to you somehow if they didn't see her on the station platform at Bekescsaba. That's the first stop on this side, I think."

"Christ, what a crazy thing to do!"

"She told them that if they *didn't* see her, it would mean she'd been arrested because she was a friend to the Romanian gipsies and was trying to help them. Whatever it was she said to them, it worked. You know what it was she wanted smuggled out of Romania, needless to say."

"How in the world should I?"

"Oh, come *on*, Ben!" Emma abruptly shuddered and put her arms round Lazenby, who had released her shoulders during her detailed explanation.

"Are you cold?"

"No, a bit scared though. Hold me."

He did so, and they clung together for a long time, before Emma moved her arms up to his neck and he felt her warm breath at his ear. Her voice was low and throaty as she whispered to him. "I've just remembered. I owe you a kiss," she said.

Eventually they broke apart, and with an arm about her waist, Lazenby steered Emma towards the other side of Castle Hill, which also boasted a rampart along which it was possible to walk, but commanded a much less glamorous view: of Budapest South railway station. They were just a few hundred yards from Lazenby's house. He had very much enjoyed kissing Emma, but told himself a little sadly that in all probability what had turned her on was not his own sex appeal, but the mistaken conviction that she had become involved in some complicated exercise in espionage, with himself cast in a James Bondish role. In the light of what she had learned, he realised that he would have to confide in her, but there were several bothersome questions to which he urgently needed answers before he was prepared to do so.

"Emma," he began in a cracked voice, then cleared

his throat and began again. "Emma, obviously I'm in no position to query what you've told me, but why on earth did the children choose you to come to with this tale, and how did they find you?"

She looked up at him with that wicked Ginger Rogers smile. "Oh, didn't I make that clear? We're old friends. Well, weeks old, anyway. I met Agnes and Sandor just a day or two after I arrived. They . . . well, I suppose you could say they picked me up during my first real stroll round Debrecen. Showed me round the shops and helped carry stuff back to my flat. And no, they didn't pick my pocket."

"But thereafter they hung around in the confident expectation of handouts, no doubt." Lazenby glared at her. "No Emma, you didn't make that clear sooner, and I strongly suspect you deliberately held that particular revelation back until now for heightened dramatic effect." He sighed and continued in a more amiable tone. "Well, at least that accounts for their knowing where you live. Tell me, did Agnes and Sandor confide in you to the extent of telling you exactly why they pursued me to Romania and kept me under what I admit sounds like expert surveillance all the while I was there?"

"Well, no. But I expect they had their reasons. I've got a lot of time for those two, Ben."

"Good grief. Well, I don't know how much Gosta Lundin paid them to smuggle her contraband over the frontier, but I hope they duly restored it to her when the train arrived in Bekescsaba."

"Oh no. They looked but couldn't see her there."

Lazenby groaned. "Ye gods! So they still have it – whatever it is."

"You're being wilfully obtuse, Ben. In the first place you know perfectly well what it is, and in the second place you ought to have gathered by now that Agnes and Sandor gave it to me. What do you think I rushed to Budapest for?"

Emma patted her shoulder bag. "It's in here."

Lazenby's head was spinning when they arrived back at the house, and he locked the front door behind them and began to mount the stone staircase to the first floor living room in silence. Emma followed, and after a few steps he felt her tug at his sleeve and thrust an envelope into his hand. It was obvious from the weight and feel of it that it contained a cassette tape in its plastic box; and with a sinking feeling mingled with relief Lazenby stowed it away in his jacket pocket as Emma began to prattle in a bright, social manner.

"It's really very kind of you to let me inflict myself on you, Ben. It'll just be the one night, of course. There are some books I simply must have for my teaching work, and they're unobtainable in Debrecen. So when Professor Horvath said I could come and try to find them here I just charged off to the station and took the next train without really thinking. I say, do you think I could possibly have a bath? I noticed you have a huge one and I've only got a shower in my flat."

"Yes, of course. You'd better let me start running it for you. There's plenty of hot water, but the tap's a bit temperamental."

One way and another, Emma had given Lazenby a great deal to think about, and he sat in one of the big armchairs in a very complicated frame of mind. The jacket was draped over the back of a straight chair against the wall and he had kicked off his shoes.

It was good to be back, at all events, and taking his ease at last at the end of such an extraordinary day. And extremely pleasant too to be able to hear distant splashing noises interspersed with snatches of song. His unexpected guest was audibly enjoying her bath. The splashing ceased, and he heard her calling out to him.

"Ben? Can you hear me, Ben?"

He went through and stood outside the bathroom door. "Yes, I'm here. Anything wrong?"

"No, it's lovely. Ben?"

"Yes?"

"Would you please wash my back for me?"

Lazenby gulped, hesitated briefly and then went in. Her hair wrapped in a turban improvised from a hand towel, Emma was sitting at one end of the huge old-fashioned tub and smiling pinkly at him. She looked happy and oddly innocent, in spite of the fact that she opened her arms in welcome. "It'll be nicer if you come in with me, Ben. There's tons of room."

"What a good idea. I'll be with you in a moment." His heart thudding with pleasure and excitement, Lazenby backed out again through the open door and swiftly undressed out of Emma's line of vision. Then he went back inside and lowered himself into the other end of the bath.

"So. Has Vishinski found the truck he's so worried about?" The KGB Deputy Resident had returned to the duty room after a few hours off, for a final late-night look round before calling it a day.

"No, Comrade. Not as of half an hour ago, at least. I've just had word from the AVH that the Englishman Lazenby has returned to his house, though. He was there briefly earlier this evening, then went out to a local restaurant with a young woman. They're back at the house now."

"I see. Well, Mr Lazenby doesn't seem to be greatly bothered, then, even though it's his truck that's gone astray."

"Very true, Comrade. AVH have activated a couple of bugs in his house, and judging by what they're picking up, they think he's enjoying a protracted and rather complicated bath with his lady friend."

Chapter Fifteen

While Lazenby and Emma sprawled in each other's arms, sleeping sweetly in the intervals of lazily sensual fondlings that sometimes developed into renewed bouts of vigorous amorous exercise, Viktor Szekacs was having a much less enjoyable time. He had been detained late into the evening at the headquarters of the *Kulturalis Kapcsolatat Intezete* or Institute of Cultural Relations, known familiarly as the KKI. When he returned there after leaving the Art Museum, the duty receptionist had passed him an urgent instruction to report without delay to the director of the Western Europe Bureau.

He did so, and found his superior in a recklessly furious mood. The fury was quite obvious, and the recklessness could easily be inferred because he was shouting at Comrade Nagy. Most of the senior staff of the KKI knew that Nagy owed his main career allegiance to the security police and that his AVH status was a great deal more elevated than that which went with his cover job in the cultural agency. They therefore treated him with wary respect, and only a first-rate crisis could have prompted the director to raise his voice to him.

As Szekacs entered the room, the director wheeled round and shouted at him too. "So here you are at last, Szekacs! About time too. Now where is this confounded truck?"

"Truck, Comrade?" Szekacs faltered, just for the sake of putting off the inevitable for a few seconds.

"Don't DARE to pretend you don't know what I'm talking about! Nagy here has just tried that on, and it was his damned boss at AVH headquarters that rang me, wanting me to explain a confused tale about an art exhibition from Romania being held up at the border and then going missing. And where do you think *he* got his information? From the SOVIET ARMY, of all people!"

Punch-drunk as he was, Szekacs understood at once why the normally insouciant Nagy looked so ill at ease, and also gathered that he had returned from Kecskemet empty-handed. The realisation made him feel sick to his empty stomach. Meantime his director was ranting on. "It's only thanks to Zsuzsa here that I've been able to find out what the hell he was on about."

With an obvious effort, he controlled himself for long enough to direct an incongruous simper at the fourth person in the room. This was Zsuzsa Ferencsik, an able young woman widely and inaccurately reputed to be a kinswoman of another Ferencsik, the eminent conductor Janos. Zsuzsa was held in general awe in the office not only on account of her supposed connections but also because of her remote, icemaiden looks and manner.

The director was so besotted with her that he could hardly bear to let her out of his sight during working hours, so she was privy to all the confidential material that passed over his desk. She may or may not have known that her boss's heart fluttered whenever he paused in his work to think about his settled ambition to make her his mistress. The poor fellow indulged in this fantasy several times a day, but it was all in vain, and not only because he suffered from halitosis and changed his shirt and underwear but once a week. Zsuzsa Ferencsik noticed the shirt and the halitosis and confidently theorised about the underwear, but these and other unsavoury aspects of the man she had to share an office with bothered her only during office hours. They didn't trouble her at other times, because she shared an apartment and was contentedly in love with a soprano soloist in the State Opera.

The news of Russian military involvement shook Szekacs to the core of his being, and had given even Nagy a nasty shock. Had they known that the Soviet Army meant, in the first instance, a Major Grigory Vishinski who was in command of little more than a glorified vehicle repair depot, they might have been marginally less agitated. On the other hand, to have known that Vishinski had a cousin highly placed in the Soviet Embassy would have scared them to death.

As it was, the immediate reaction of each of them was to try to defend himself at the expense of the other. They accordingly launched into a pointless squabble under Zsuzsa's cool eye, trading increasingly intemperate accusations of sole responsibility for the failure to meet Lazenby's convoy at the border crossing near Szeged. With worries enough of his own to occupy his mind, the director paid scant attention, and soon raised a hand so forbiddingly that the gesture shut them both up.

"Enough!" he said sharply, having slowly recovered something approaching composure. "It will in due course become necessary to establish the truth about which of you is primarily to blame for this extraordinary piece of inefficiency. At present, however, I have a more pressing concern. A very large Bulgarian-registered truck with a driver of the same nationality, and containing a large number of valuable British paintings has, if I am to believe you, disappeared off the face of the earth, somewhere between Kecskemet and here. That is no great distance. Forty-five minutes at most by road. You say you have searched for it, Nagy. Why have you failed to find it?"

Nagy raised his hands in a gesture that culminated in his pointing a finger at Szekacs. It was quite effective in communicating his meaning, which he emphasised in words. "Don't ask me. I'm just a driver. Ask him."

The director turned to Szekacs. "Well?"

"I don't know, Comrade Director."

"Yet you say you've telephoned Lazenby and told him everything's under control. What possessed you to do such an idiotic thing when you are both manifestly floundering about at a complete loss?"

"Comrade, he threatened to ask his ambassador to make a formal complaint to the Ministry of Foreign Affairs, and to request them put the matter in the hands of the police."

"Oh. Did he?"

"Yes."

"*Jesusz Maria!*"

"It seemed to me that we ought to avoid that if we possibly can. So I bought us some time. After my phone call to him, Lazenby won't take any action before tomorrow at the earliest. I'm supposed to meet him at the Art Gallery at ten. We'll surely have been able to trace the vehicle before then. If not, I suppose I could even fob Lazenby off again somehow: tell him the rest of the paintings have already been unloaded and taken inside."

"Don't be ridiculous." The director put his face very close to his subordinate's and glared at him. Szekacs closed his eyes and tried manfully to disregard the awful smell of his breath. "You and Nagy have lost this truck between you. You have over twelve hours in which to find it and deliver the paintings to the museum. I don't care how you do it, in fact I don't want to know. I'm leaving now, and I expect to have a positive report and a full written explanation of how the pair of you brought about this fiasco waiting for me eight-thirty tomorrow morning."

The director strode over to the door of his office and wrenched it open, then pointed outwards in the manner of a Victorian father turning a seduced daughter out of the house with her shameful bundle. Nagy and Szekacs shuffled past him and disappeared from view, though their voices could be heard as they renewed their squabbling in the corridor. He closed the door and smiled sadly at his secretary. "I'm sincerely sorry that you had to witness that scene, Zsuzsa," he murmured in what he believed to be a sexy voice.

Zsuzsa shrugged elegantly. "I shall take two hours off tomorrow in lieu of overtime," she said, and her boss nodded meekly.

"Yes, yes. Of course."

After a while, Nagy and Szekacs came to their senses and realised that recriminations would have to be deferred, and that they had no option but to make common cause. A few minutes later they set out together in the Chaika to search the road to Kecskemet once more.

They stopped at every garage and other establishment where the Bulgarian driver might have parked his vehicle, and peered into such workshops as were still open for business late in the evening, quizzing the staff on duty with a complete lack of success. They finally reached Kecskemet at about the time Lazenby was clambering into the bath with Emma Jarvis at her invitation.

Two hours later Szekacs was sitting miserably in the office of the night duty inspector in Kecskemet police headquarters while Nagy was closeted with the AVH liaison officer. Someone had given him a sticky bun and bottle of a bright orange soft drink, but by that time his misery was so profound that he had almost forgotten how hungry he was.

Had they still been on duty, Sergeant Hunyadi or his underling might have been moved to give the men from Budapest an edited account of the incident at the bridge. It was however after midnight, Hunyadi hadn't reported the matter, and both officers were now tucked up in bed, in more respectable and very much less exciting circumstances than Lazenby and Emma.

Szekacs realised glumly that he could do nothing further himself, and accepted that Comrade Nagy was effectively in charge. Unlike himself, Nagy could pull strings, possibly arrange for a full-scale police search operation on some specious security grounds, invoke the shadowy powers that employed him, do *something* to extricate them from the appalling mess they were in . . .

Chapter Sixteen

Lazenby stretched luxuriously, aware that something very nice had happened, but unable for a split second to remember exactly what it was. After a few moments he opened his eyes, and delicious recollections flooded into his consciousness at the sight of Emma sleeping at his side, a lock of her hair plastered to her temple.

Reaching out a cautious hand, he rested it gently on a warm breast, thinking how wonderful it would be if he could only stay like that for the rest of his life. He smiled to himself, blinked a few times, and then leapt out of bed in a panic as his eye fell on the alarm clock on the bedside table. It showed seven forty-two, and Rozsika was due to arrive at eight.

He hurried to the bathroom and prepared himself for a new day in about three minutes flat, then scrambled on a few clothes and, at ten minutes to eight, went back to Emma. His imitation of a startled faun must have awakened her, because, though she was looking as dazed and sated as he still felt, her eyes were open. Focusing them on him, she regarded him tenderly. Lazenby tried to keep any note of urgency out of his voice.

"Dearest Emma, good morning, and I thank you with all my heart."

Her arms reached out to him. "Mmmm. Oh Ben, it was *great*! It really did happen, didn't it? Why don't you take those boring clothes off and come back to bed?"

He groaned dramatically. "How I wish I could! But duty

calls. And I'm afraid I have to disturb you too. There's no need for you to get up, but if you wouldn't mind it'd be better if you move to the bed in the spare room. My housekeeper will probably turn up at any minute, and . . ."

In a moment a warm and naked Emma was out of bed and in his arms, hugging him violently. "All right, you heartless beast. I'll go and mess up the other bed and get dressed. But only on condition that I can come back tonight. Because I've just remembered that tomorrow's Sunday."

"Whatever you say." Lazenby admired her neat little bottom as Emma skipped past him, and went into the kitchen to make some coffee. Rozsika had her own key to the front door, because she normally arrived after he had left for the Embassy, and left again early in the afternoon. The house was less than fifteen minutes drive away from the Embassy, and he often lunched at home, alone or with one, two or at most three guests. Rozsika's *entrée* repertoire was uninspired, running to little beyond chicken paprika, beef gulyas or stuffed cabbage, but most of the people he took home to sample her cooking marvelled at the scrumptious apple strudel or delicate *millefeuille* she produced to go with coffee afterwards.

Rozsika was a few minutes late that day, and it was at a little before eight-ten that Lazenby heard the great door downstairs creak open and her step on the stair. By that time Emma was dressed, and they were both sitting sedately at the kitchen table drinking coffee.

It wasn't the first time that a lone female guest had stayed overnight under Lazenby's roof. His sister Jemima, five years younger than he and looking even in casual clothes every inch the brisk marketing executive she was, had made a short holiday visit a month or two after his arrival at post; and Emma's counterpart from the university at Szeged, a hearty person who was towards the end of her three-year contract, had stayed on two occasions. The daughter of an archdeacon, Laura Weldon would have roared with laughter if Lazenby had so much as made a flirtatiously gallant remark to her; not that he had been remotely tempted to do any such thing.

There had been male house guests as well: a poet who had been sent from Britain under the terms of the Cultural Agreement to read his own work at the Writers' Union and was nervous about staying in what he referred to as "communist pubs", and yet another contract lecturer, a burly fellow who was assigned to Pecs and who turned up uninvited on Lazenby's doorstep from time to time to complain about his salary and conditions of service, drink his reluctant host's whisky and hold forth about the experimental novel he was writing until he ostensibly realised with a start that he was far too pissed even to think about setting out on the two-hour drive back to Pecs before morning.

So Rozsika was not unaccustomed to finding cuckoos either male or female in the Lazenby nest, and hadn't batted an eyelid when she first saw Jemima breakfasting with him, even before she learned that the elegant lady was her temporary employer's sister. Laura Weldon was of course *sui generis* and hardly likely to occasion prurient speculation anyway. Lazenby had invited other women to the house with intent to dally, and they had cooperated with varying degrees of enthusiasm, but none of these had still been on the premises at breakfast time. Perhaps for that reason he was shy about letting Rozsika meet Emma, and therefore greeted her with somewhat excessive joviality when she appeared in the kitchen doorway.

"Ah, Rozsika! *Jo napot kivanok!*"

"*Jo napot*, Lazenby-*Ur*."

Lazenby introduced Emma, who had a trace of marmalade on her chin and looked delicious in Lazenby's opinion; and Rozsika acknowledged her with frosty politeness. She was frowning, but not apparently over Emma's presence.

"You're back, then. Will you be wanting lunch today?" Rozsika then said in the slow, clearly articulated Hungarian she used in speaking to Lazenby. Without waiting for him to reply, she thrust a folded scrap of paper at him. "I found this in your letter box," she said accusingly. "Looks like English. For you, is it?"

Lazenby reached out and took the paper from her. It was coarse and undyed, and looked as if it had been torn off one of the cone-shaped bags grudgingly made up by market women from cheap wrapping paper when Lazenby bought vegetables or fruit without having taken his own shopping bag with him. It was roughly rectangular, about three inches by four, and bore a pencilled note written in childish, misshapen capital letters:

TOMORO 11 HOUR HORTOBAGY AGNES

Lazenby stared at the paper stupidly, then quickly crumpled it up and stuffed it in his pocket before Emma could see what was written on it. "Oh, that's okay, Rozsika," he blurted out in English before switching to Hungarian, in which it was difficult for him to affect nonchalance. "It's just a note from a friend who called while I was out."

Rozsika sniffed. "Lunch today?" she repeated.

"No, I don't think so, thank you." Rozsika nodded curtly and bustled off. Emma, who been quietly getting on with her toast and marmalade, looked at Lazenby quizzically.

"She's a formidable old battleaxe, isn't she," she murmured. "What was all that about? I mean, the piece of paper she gave you?"

"Paper? Oh, *that*. Not important. Listen, I'm afraid you'll have to fend for yourself at lunchtime, unless you'd like me to ask Rozsika to fix some for you here. I shall have to be off to the Embassy in a little while."

"Don't worry about lunch, I'll find something while I'm out. Will you give me a lift as far as the Embassy, though?"

"Gladly – oh Christ, excuse me a minute." Lazenby had abruptly remembered that his jacket with the envelope containing Gosta's tape was still in the living room where he had left it the previous night, and he shot out of his chair to go and fetch it before Rozsika found it when putting his jacket away. It was bad enough that she'd seen the cryptic note from Agnes.

Emma watched him rush out of the kitchen, and smiled happily to herself. Ben Lazenby wasn't at all bad in bed, but she knew that what really excited her was the idea of sleeping with a spy. She didn't quite know how she would use the rest of her free day in Budapest, but fully intended to begin by begging a ride with Ben as far as the British Embassy and then going to look at the chic boutiques of Vaci Utca, several of which presumably dealt in filmy lingerie suitable for a secret agent's mistress. It would be quite wrong to be reclining on Ben's chaise longue in underwear from British Home Stores when he arrived home that evening.

Left alone in the house, Rozsika set to work to make the beds and clean the house with her customary vigour, but in a thoughtful mood. She quite liked Lazenby, and was glad that he seemed to have acquired a nice new lady friend. A youngish divorced man needed a bit of a cuddle, and Rozsika wouldn't mind admitting that she'd not be averse to providing him with something of the kind herself on an occasional or even a regular basis. He either didn't fancy her, though, or more likely had been warned off. Rozsika paused in her labours to admire her buxom reflection in the mirrored door of the wardrobe. Not bad for forty-eight, she considered, and Lazenby-*Ur* would probably be surprised to discover what a good time she could give him. Oh well, never mind, the pair of them had evidently been enjoying themselves. It was tactful of this young woman to have amateurishly rumpled the bed in the spare room, even though it was perfectly obvious that she hadn't slept in it.

A professor from Debrecen, he'd said. Fancy that! Well, he was safely back from Romania, anyway, and that was something. What a silly old fool she was, to have worried about him after watching him leave on Monday in the company of those two unsavoury specimens from the KKI, neither of whom she would trust farther than she could throw him. Oh dear, though, what about this note in the letter box? She almost wished now that she hadn't copied the few words of the message on to a bit of paper of her own. She didn't mind rummaging through his things, or turning in the crumpled papers he left in his waste-paper basket: she valued her job and knew very well that if she wanted to continue to enjoy the perks that went with it she had to show willing and provide convincing evidence that she kept her eyes open.

Thinking about perks reminded her to go into the bathroom and put out a fresh bar of the Camay soap he kept in the cupboard there. She wrapped up the half used one in lavatory paper to take home with her, and while she was at it helped herself to a thick wodge of Kleenex paper handkerchiefs. Then, before it slipped her mind, she went into the kitchen and tipped a good handful of coffee beans into a plastic bag, stowing all her loot in her capacious handbag. At that point she thought she'd earned a cup of coffee, and warmed up the good cupful remaining in the pot.

Hortobagy. She'd never been there, but everybody knew where it was and had heard of the famous Hortobagy pancakes. She must make them for Lazenby-Ur some time. So somebody called Agnes was apparently arranging to meet him there. Who could Agnes be, and why had she used such a grubby bit of paper? The letters and notes her employer left about the house were always written on paper of a quality rarely seen by ordinary people, much less used. It was just possible that this woman Agnes really was a foreign friend of his who came to the door expecting to find him in, and getting no answer when she rang the bell had been obliged to scribble a hurried note on whatever she could lay her hand on.

On the other hand, the writing itself had been very peculiar. Rozsika was no scholar, but she knew an educated hand when she saw one, and she also knew more English than she let on. TOMORO could possibly be a jazzy American spelling like TONITE, but it seemed unlikely. No, the unknown woman who was presumably expecting to meet Lazenby in the Hortobagy region at 11 "tomoro", or possibly informing him that something was going to happen there at that time, was most likely a Hungarian, and a poorly schooled one at that.

Intrigued, Rozsika wondered afresh who on earth this Agnes could be. Was she perhaps one of the whores who hung about in the bar at the Astoria Hotel hoping to pick up foreigners? They were up to all the tricks, including chalking their prices both in forints and dollars on the soles of their shoes so that when crossing their legs they could offer not only a glimpse of the goods but also advertise their cost. Rozsika giggled to herself and shook her head. No, it was hardly possible that a senior diplomat already having it off with a classy English lady professor would allow himself to be seen picking up a tart in the bar at the Astoria. In any case, why go all the way to Hortobagy? She shrugged. Oh well, she was due to look in at the office after work that afternoon. There was plenty of time before then to decide whether or not to report the matter of the note as well as telling them about the young lady from Debrecen.

* * *

After bidding Emma a fond farewell at the reserved parking area round the corner from the Embassy and promising to meet her at the Very Smarty Café at five o'clock, Lazenby strolled up to the double doors of the British Embassy for the first time that week, feeling as if he had been away for at least a month. He nodded affably at the uniformed Hungarian security policeman on duty in his little sentry box outside, and waved up at the third-floor window in the office building on the other side of the street where, it was generally believed, the authorities posted a man with a camera to take pictures of all visitors to the Embassy.

Lazenby was feeling pretty good about life, on the whole. He wished it hadn't been Rozsika who came across the mysterious note in his letter box, and even more that Agnes hadn't written it at all. The last thing he planned to do was go on some wild goose chase to Hortobagy at her bidding, even if she had delivered Gosta's tape to Emma. On the other hand the said tape would soon be locked away in his confidential filing cabinet in the safety of the Embassy, and would stay there until such time as he could hand it back to Gosta.

Above all, in an hour or so he would go to the art museum, see the remaining paintings for himself and get the wretched things signed for; and later keep his tryst with the gratifyingly enthusiastic Emma before taking her home with him.

Chapter Seventeen

"Well, we've found the driver." Slumped in a chair that seemed to have been deliberately designed to deny any human occupant the prospect of ease, and somewhere between a hideous parody of sleep and half-consciousness, Viktor Szekacs failed to register what was being said to him until Comrade Nagy seized him by the shoulders and shook him roughly. Szekacs whimpered in misery and made feeble and completely ineffectual swatting movements with his hands as he came to, but it was only when Nagy almost bellowed at him that he came to something approaching life.

"I SAID WE'VE FOUND THE DRIVER!"

"Driver?" Given that he could not remember where he was, and felt as if death would be a happy release, it was a considerable achievement on Szekacs's part to have uttered even a single word, but Nagy seemed far from impressed.

"Yes, *driver*. The Bulgarian driver. Remember why we're here? Pull yourself together, for Christ's sake!"

Szekacs blinked, rubbed his bleary eyes and tried to stand up, wincing as his aching muscles protested. Temporarily abandoning the attempt, he struggled into a reasonably upright sitting position, ran a furry tongue over his teeth and rolled his head about as he tried to obey. After a second or two he remembered that he was in a poky little office in Kecskemet police headquarters, and saw that the first light of dawn was visible in what little of the sky he could see through the grimy window.

At last he managed a ghastly smile. "Have you really found the truck, Comrade? Oh, well done!"

"I didn't say anything about the truck. I said we've found the driver."

Szekacs gazed at him stupidly, his mouth open.

"He was picked up several hours ago outside a boozer in Szolnok. No papers, and mumbling in a foreign lingo. The local cops thought he was drunk out of his skull and put him in the slammer to sober up. It wasn't until we put out a confidential alert on our own network that some bright spark put two and two together and tried Russian on him. All they've been able to get out of him so far is some pack of lies about being hijacked by gipsies."

"Gipsies? In *Szolnok*?"

Comrade Nagy raised his eyes to heaven in a manner of which his priestly brother-in-law would surely have approved. "Yes, Szolnok. There are gipsies all over the place. Wake up, you stupid ponce!"

Szekacs was still having difficulty in tuning in to the right wavelength. "But . . . but Szolnok is nowhere near here."

"What's that got to do with it? Besides, it isn't all that far away. There's no direct road, but it'll only take me about an hour to drive there and find out for myself what the hell the stupid peasant's got to say for himself. I'm taking the Chaika. You'd better get back to the office and cook up some story while I organise a search for the truck in the vicinity of Szolnok." Nagy looked at his watch, a heavy Russian model which itself had something of a Chaika look about it. "It's getting on for five. I'm told the first train into Pest leaves at a quarter to six."

Szekacs had struggled to his feet while Nagy was holding forth, and, swaying slightly, peered at him belligerently. "*What* was it you called me a while ago, Comrade?"

"A stupid ponce, *Comrade*. And so you are. It's time you grasped that I've taken charge. Somebody's got to find this bloody vehicle, and you couldn't find your way out of a wet paper bag. I'll ring you at the KKI at about seven-thirty."

Nagy stormed out of the room, leaving Szekacs opening and shutting his mouth like a stranded fish.

Lazenby nodded and smiled at Gaby, the locally-engaged Grade 4 receptionist who dealt with the small number of Hungarian citizens who called at the Embassy, handing out visa application forms to those with permission to travel to Britain, and British Tourist Association posters to the occasional teacher of English who braved the stern scrutiny of the security policeman outside. Gaby was a comfortably built, motherly-looking woman who had an embarrassing habit of describing all her symptoms in detail when asked how she was. Since these were usually of an intimate gynaecological nature, Lazenby had learned to harden his heart and pass straight through to the inner regions of the building, where the approach to the chancery proper was guarded night and day by one of the several British security officers on the Embassy staff.

"Morning, Bob."

"Morning, Mr L. Haven't seen you lately." The security guard produced a key and with it unlocked a shallow wall cupboard beside his desk. Inside were rows of hooks, from about half of which hung keys on rings, each with a numbered red plastic tag. He handed one of the rings to Lazenby. It had two keys on it.

"No. Been out of town for a few days. Thanks." Duly logged in and mounting the stairs to his office, Lazenby was conscious of being glad to be back. After unlocking the door to his room and closing it behind him, he briefly pondered the question of where to keep Gosta's tape. The second key on his ring was to the filing cabinet in which he kept such papers as the British Council sent to him under privacy markings: all classified Embassy files were stored in the registry.

The bulk of the contents of the filing cabinet were far from being either confidential or even interesting, consisting of routine unclassified files, the British Council's published annual reports for the past several years, the bulky and largely incomprehensible Financial Handbook with a large stack of amendments Lazenby hadn't got round to incorporating, and a number of ringing pronouncements about the way ahead produced by the Council's management advisers.

Among the detritus littering the bottoms of the three metal drawers underneath the hanging cardboard dividers were a giveaway British Airways calendar for 1980, an assortment of bulldog clips, a few of the 1981 British Council Christmas cards, and yes, a miscellany of cassette tapes, some single, some in boxed sets. All had been sent out by the Music Department in the sporadic fits of generosity which occasionally seized them towards the end of a financial year when they had money to burn. Lazenby and his predecessors had taken home the more attractive recordings, leaving the more recondite to gather dust.

Contemplating them, it seemed to Lazenby that even if a diplomatic colleague on night security duty were to take it into his or her head to investigate his room in search of classified material not properly stowed away, and was so caddish as to examine the contents of his filing cabinet, a tape recording purporting to be of new work by Harrison Birtwistle would hardly attract particular attention. He therefore opened the envelope Emma had brought from Debrecen, removed the tape from the unlabelled box inside and performed a switch, so that Ceauşescu's indiscretions nestled in a Birtwistle box and Birtwistle languished, undraped as it were, underneath a small pile of blank medical and dental expenses claim forms.

Lazenby looked at his watch. He really ought to go and fill up his in-tray with the pile of papers that would be waiting for him in his pigeonhole in the registry, but it was already nine and he was due at the art gallery to meet Dracula at ten. He would need to leave the Embassy again in half an hour, perhaps just popping his head round Loo Brush's door on the way out to thank him sarcastically for all his help on the telephone the previous morning. He therefore sat at his empty desk and puzzled over the note that Rozsika had handed him.

His telephone rang three or four minutes later.

"Good *morning*, Svetlana Ivanova." The duty KGB officer straightened up in his chair in what he thought of as a lazily insolent manner when the Deputy Resident sailed into the communications room. A macho type, he detested having a woman in authority over him. It was particularly galling at times like this, when the Resident was away and she was in charge. It was his habit then to address her in terms of exaggerated and sugary politeness, which he believed to convey his contempt for her.

"Good morning. I left word last night that I was to be advised if there were any significant developments in the matter of the Bulgarian truck that the Assistant Military Attaché reported missing yesterday." She yawned lazily. "I was not disturbed overnight, so I presume that nothing came in during your shift."

"I'm so very glad you slept well, Svetlana Ivanova. There *was* a development two or three hours ago, but it was hardly significant, and I couldn't bring myself to disturb your rest over it."

The Deputy Resident looked at him sharply, on the point of rebuking him, but was then struck by the cringing unctuousness of his manner. He wasn't a bad-looking fellow, and in the few weeks since he had been posted to the residency she had gained a distinct impression that he was rather sweet on her. His frequent use of her name was rather touching. "Yes, well, Comrade, let me be the judge of its significance. What's happened?"

"You're not angry with me, then?"

She smiled roguishly. "I might be, if you keep me waiting too long."

"Well, the AVH reported a couple of hours ago that the driver of the truck is in police custody in Szolnok. But they haven't been able to trace his vehicle yet. I'm sure they've been doing their very best, Svetlana Ivanova."

"I see. Give me the tape of the telephone call. I'll listen to it and then have a word with AVH myself." She looked down at the smirking young man. "And incidentally . . . oh, never mind." She took the tape he handed her and went through to her own office. The duty officer watched her go, noting her high colour and satisfied that he had well and truly shown the silly old cow how thoroughly he despised her.

In the privacy of her office the Deputy Resident smiled to herself. It was rather naughty of him to keep her in the dark even for a couple of hours, but no great harm done. There was no doubt about it, the young man was completely smitten. It might be amusing to invite him to her apartment for drinks one evening soon . . .

She listened to the recording of the short, matter-of-fact telephone message from the Hungarian security police, and then reached for her own telephone. Hijacked by *gipsies*? Extraordinary, if true, and one had to ask oneself why. A sensible first step would be to get in touch with the Bulgarian Embassy. Her opposite number there – though of course it was laughable to equate a mere First Secretary (Political) with a KGB colonel – might know the answer. If he did, she thought she could persuade him to reveal it to her.

*   *   *

"Is that Mr Lazenby?" The voice at the other end of the line was faint and sounded uncertain.

"Yes. That you, Viktor? You sound a bit strange. Nothing wrong, I hope? I was just about to set out for the gallery."

"Yes. No, I mean no, nothing is wrong, but yes, this is Szekacs, calling from the Institute. The, ah, museum authorities have just been in communication with me to advise me that the responsible curator is unwell, and that in the circumstances they would prefer to postpone the unpacking of the paintings until next Monday, when the gallery is in any case closed to the public – "

"*Monday*? Damn it all, Viktor, the exhibition's due to be opened by my Ambassador and your Minister of Culture on Wednesday!"

"They are confident that there will be more than enough time, Mr Lazenby."

"Listen, Viktor, the rest of the paintings have shown up, haven't they?"

"There is absolutely no need for you to worry on that score, Mr Lazenby. I look forward to meeting you at the gallery on Monday at ten in the morning. Now please excuse me, for I have a great deal to do."

Lazenby kept the receiver in his hand and gaped at it long after he heard the click. The bugger had hung up on him. "No need for you to worry on that score," he'd said. In a pig's ear. The one thing Szekacs hadn't said, either the previous evening or just now, was that the missing truck and its contents had been found and taken to the gallery. He slowly replaced the receiver and put both hands up to his head.

A few hundred yards away Szekacs slowly replaced *his* receiver and put both hands up to *his* head. Would this nightmare never end? His body was slick with stale sweat, he needed a shave as well as a shower and a change of clothes, and the first train from Kecskemet had been so packed with early shift workers that he'd had to stand all the way. Nagy had kept his promise to ring from Szolnok at seven thirty, but had nothing of comfort to report, and had chuckled cruelly when urging Szekacs to go easy on the Director. The Director hadn't in fact turned up yet, but Szekacs knew that the summons couldn't be long delayed. What he really needed to do was sleep for about twelve hours, but in the meantime a cup of proper coffee at Gerbaud's might keep him from bursting into tears of misery and frustration.

Emma Jarvis happened to be passing on the other side of Disz Square when a dishevelled man lurched out of the building opposite, almost next door to the big record and music shop. She knew it to house the offices of the KKI, because she'd been taken there herself when she first arrived in Hungary, to complete the complicated paperwork involved in taking up her contract to teach in Debrecen. Almost immediately she recognised the man as Viktor Szekacs, but a Szekacs in even more terrible shape than the pale, fraught man who had brought Ben to call on Professor Horvath at the University at the beginning of the week, and a far cry indeed from the supercilious *apparatchik* she had met originally.

He looked pitiful: apparently so sunk in private misery that Emma thought it in the highest degree unlikely that he would notice her. So she paused and watched as he tottered off, and then followed at a discreet distance until she saw him enter the stately patisserie and coffee shop where she was herself to meet her new and exciting lover at the end of the day.

It was all very exciting.

Chapter Eighteen

Lazenby was so disturbed by the call from Szekacs that he decided to go to the gallery anyway and try to find out for himself whether or not the other half of the exhibition had materialised. Not wishing to draw attention to himself by using his car with its tell-tale number plates, he found a taxi and asked to be dropped off at the entrance to the zoo, a short walk from his real destination.

Making his way as unobtrusively as possible to the back of the art gallery, he saw that the high concertina doors to the service entrance were closed and heavily padlocked. A good or a bad sign? Impossible to know, but at all events there was no Bulgarian lorry parked in the vicinity.

Lazenby spared a thought for Boris. Back in the golden days of what had in the last twenty-four hours come to seem like the remote past, when he was in occasional elementary communication with both drivers, it hadn't occurred to him to ask them whither they were bound after delivering the paintings in Budapest. Back to base, he rather supposed, though almost immediately he went on to argue with himself. Such relatively sophisticated vehicles must represent a significant capital asset for the state road transport agency they were assigned to, and its managers would presumably not want them to be driven without paid-for loads any further than was absolutely essential.

Lazenby surreptitiously crossed his fingers. It might simply have been Dracula's inherent deviousness combined with professional caution about what he said over insecure telephone lines that had made his utterances so worryingly ambiguous. The first of his two calls had, after all, been comparatively early the previous evening. The errant Ivan with his lorry might well have arrived at the museum by then and the custom-built, blue-painted wooden crates with their valuable contents have been off-loaded and safely entrusted to the care of the gallery authorities. Reunited with Boris and no doubt with a lot to talk about during refreshment stops, Ivan and his colleague could have departed for their next destination no more than a few hours late. To pick up a cargo of electrical appliances in Vienna, for example, or of sprouts in Brussels.

The art museum was open that day, and Lazenby thought he would exercise his right as a member of the public to buy a ticket and wander through the galleries. He nourished the faint hope that while so doing he might come across one of the curatorial staff he already knew by sight, and seize the opportunity for a brief exchange of courtesies. Such a person could with a word set his mind at rest once and for all. He therefore made his way up the great stone steps and into the impressive main entrance; reassured to see a poster announcing that an exhibition entitled "Two Hundred Years of British Landscape Painting" was due to open the following Wednesday and to be displayed for a full month. The gallery's administrators clearly still thought it was going to happen, and they should know.

Lazenby wandered about aimlessly for about a quarter of an hour, seeing nobody other than the uniformed, mostly female attendants, a few individual gallery-goers and an attentive flock of well-scrubbed schoolchildren trailing round in the wake of an excruciatingly jolly and loquacious museum guide while the teacher in charge of the party kept them under her eagle eye.

He was staring absent-mindedly at a depiction in the

heroic style of a battle scene involving Turks and Magyars, and wondering if he should force the issue by going to the office and asking to see somebody in authority, when he felt a light touch on his shoulder which made him start violently and his heart pound. Whirling round with a poorly-stifled gasp, he found himself face to face with Gosta Lundin.

"Hello, dear Ben! Goodness, you do look startled!"

At the sight of the Finnish woman Lazenby experienced a vivid recollection of their parting in Romania less than forty-eight hours previously, and he was both glad to see her safe and well and at the same time ashamed. For Gosta had uncomplainingly accepted his cowardly refusal to help her: even kissing him goodbye before striding bravely into the unknown to persist in her dangerous attempt to frustrate an evil plan.

Whereas what had he done? Put her more or less out of his mind while he worried about his career, for God's sake! The crucial tape recording had been to him merely an inconvenience; its only incidental merit residing in the fact that his connection with it had fired Emma Jarvis's imagination so much that she had blatantly invited him to make love to her. Lazenby had seldom liked himself less, and he did his best to avoid Gosta's eye.

"Gosta. Thank God you're safe," he mumbled. "What on earth are you doing here of all places?"

She shrugged. "Well, I thought I might find you here today. I expected you to be very busy supervising the arrangements for your exhibition."

"Ah. Well, as you can see, I'm not. At the moment, anyway." He glanced up at her, then lowered his eyes again. "You had no trouble getting across the border from Arad, it seems."

"Not so much, no. The Romanian border guards searched me and my suitcase very thoroughly, but they didn't find anything their colleagues overlooked when they had a peek at my things while we were in that restaurant on the way. And my papers were in order, as I told you. I came here in the hope of seeing you, Ben. I'm sorry, but again I want to ask your help."

"I let you down badly last time. I'm surprised you think it's worth trying again." The note purporting to be from Agnes was in Lazenby's wallet in the inside breast pocket of his suit jacket, and he was so conscious of its presence that he half-expected it to burn a hole in the rather expensive Austin Reed suit he'd bought when last in London. He looked about and, seeing that they were the only people in the large room apart from the attendant and two art lovers well separated from each other and that none of the three was within earshot, lowered his voice. "So you didn't personally try to smuggle anything into Hungary, after all."

"No, Ben. And as I told you, I didn't hide it in your car, either." Gosta spoke quietly.

"I know." Lazenby allowed a hint of disillusionment into his voice, and Gosta looked puzzled. Then she spoke hesitantly.

"I'm still looking forward to our date, Ben. I really am. I want to go to dinner with you at, oh, the Matyas Pince restaurant . . . and then maybe back to your place?"

Lazenby's throat felt dry, and he swallowed hard. "Lovely idea," he managed to croak bitterly before having to swallow again. "I'll be able to hand your property back to you. It was clever of you if a bit dangerous to entrust it to those gipsy children." To his surprise she laughed heartily.

"Dear Ben, you're so sweet. As if I would do such a thing! No, no, that wasn't the real tape. I gave that – oh, dear God, no . . ." The laughter drained from her expression as she stared fixedly over Lazenby's shoulder, and then everything seemed to happen very quickly.

The attendant got up from her straight wooden chair in

the corner of the room but stood still, her eyes on the two male visitors who had previously seemed to have nothing to do with each other. One was wearing a sober suit, the other casual clothes, but there was no longer any doubt that they had a common purpose as they strode side by side towards Gosta. The tinted glasses they had both put on gave them a sinister, menacing look, but it was the one in the suit who addressed her, and he did so in polite Hungarian.

"Please come with us, madam."

Still confused, and taken aback as he was by this latest unexpected turn of events, Lazenby nevertheless acted with some presence of mind, whipping out his diplomatic identity card and holding it open in front of the man's face.

"I am the Cultural Attaché at the British Embassy, and this lady is with me. I wish to know who you are and what you want with her." His halting Hungarian seemed to be comprehensible to the man, who continued in that language.

"We know who you are. Unlike you, this lady has no diplomatic immunity, and our business with her is not your concern."

Gosta's face was pale and she looked terrified, but when she turned to Lazenby and spoke to him in English, her voice was under control. "Thank you for trying to help, Ben, but it's no good arguing with them. Will you inform my Embassy and Reuters, please . . . and if there are any, er, *messages*, please do what you can about them. You understand, I think." She blinked and smiled at the same time, and then turned and addressed her abductors in correct Hungarian. "I take it that you are agents of either the Hungarian or the Romanian security service."

The one who seemed to be in charge stood as still as if he had been frozen solid as Gosta continued. "This gentleman showed you his credentials. May I see yours, please?" There was a tense silence for a few seconds, before the man shrugged; after which he produced from his pocket and briefly showed her a warrant card which bore what Lazenby recognised at once as the official Hungarian government crest.

"We do not permit Romanian security officials to operate in our country," he said stiffly, and the disgust in his voice persuaded Lazenby that he was an authentic Hungarian.

"Very well. I agree to accompany you voluntarily," Gosta said in a small voice. She directed a strange little smile at Lazenby and turned towards the door, and the attendant stood stiffly to attention while the ill-assorted trio passed her.

The attendant was still watching them and was blocking the doorway as Lazenby followed, so that he had to edge his way out of the room sideways. Keeping the other three in view, he went down the main stairs after them in time to see them disappear through a door marked STAFF ONLY. Clearly, the men were on the premises with the knowledge of the gallery authorities.

Quickening his pace, Lazenby made his way out of the building and hurried round to the rear, where he knew the service entrance to be and thought he remembered seeing a separate door for staff use. His hunch was confirmed: there was a staff entrance, and moreover a nondescript car was parked beside it with its engine running and a watchful man at the wheel. Having already declared his identity to the two men he was sure were AVH goons, Lazenby saw no need to skulk about furtively at that stage. He therefore took up a position about two yards in front of the car and stared pointedly at its driver.

It required a good deal of self-control to maintain an appearance of patient impassivity, because his thoughts were in complete turmoil. Why, if the men were indeed Hungarian agents, should they arrest Gosta, a "friendly" Finnish national? If the Hungarians had anything against her, surely they could easily have arranged for her to be denied entry, or even had her arrested at the frontier?

In any case, where were they taking her? The days of staged show trials were long past in Hungary at least, where the regime now deployed much subtler ways of pressurising potential dissidents into compliance with its policies. Thumbscrews and electric shocks were out, having been replaced by an effective combination of incentives and not-very-frightening but nevertheless real threats. Thus, a teacher or public official who showed a degree of commitment and worked with due diligence might be granted a holiday package in the Soviet Union. A really fervent supporter of the system or a gifted musician or writer could look forward to a trip to Yugoslavia or even western Europe.

On the other hand, people who attended the annual rally at the foot of the statue of Sandor Petofi on the embankment of the Danube to celebrate the poet's birthday, thus declaring themselves to be malcontents, were warned that their jobs or promotion prospects would be jeopardised if there was any repetition of such impudence. Those who went so far as to make impromptu speeches to the assembled crowd were liable to summary arrest and a jail sentence.

The nearest thing to a legal public protest against the regime was made every Sunday at the end of the ten o'clock High Mass at the Matthew Church, the only regular public occasion when people were permitted to sing the *Hymnus*, the pre-revolutionary national anthem as set by the composer Erkel. No Catholic, Lazenby often walked to the church from his house at about eleven simply to experience the *frisson* that united the congregation, and the intense fervour that became almost palpable as soon as the introductory chords were played on the organ and by the small orchestra in the gallery, and to listen to the full-throated congregational singing that bore the admittedly rather banal and soupy tune along on surging waves of yearning passion. The *Hymnus* invariably made Lazenby come out in goose pimples all over.

So, Hungary in 1982 was still a police state, but one in which the crude excesses generally associated with dictatorships were so tempered that most observers considered it comparatively benign on the whole. That made Gosta Lundin's arrest, for all the courageous dignity of her behaviour, all the more frightening to Lazenby.

His thoughts tumbling about chaotically, Lazenby stood there facing the AVH car without really seeing it, and the fixity of his apparent gaze must have had an unnerving effect on its driver. All at once Lazenby was jolted back into awareness of his surroundings by the sound of the slamming of the car door and an angry Hungarian expletive. "Get out of here!"

"I beg your pardon?"

"I said get out of my way. What do you think you're up to?" The driver was a young man, probably still in his twenties, and Lazenby surveyed him from the top of his closely shorn head to his feet, shod in cracked plastic shoes.

"I'm waiting for a friend, comrade. Who are you waiting for? Oh dear, you seem to have forgotten to put your handbrake on properly." The car was in fact inching backwards on the very slight slope, and Lazenby stepped forward and gave the front a gentle shove, as a result of which it rolled back several feet, gathering speed as it did so. The young man gave an audible yelp of dismay and, directing a glance of pure hatred at Lazenby, ran after it and wrenched at the passenger door, falling over his feet in the process.

It was at this moment that the staff door opened and Gosta emerged with her captors.

Emma Jarvis stepped out of the lingerie boutique in Vaci

Utca well pleased with her purchases and thanking her lucky stars that she had been able to use her American Express card. It wasn't surprising to see the blue sign outside restaurants and the up-market stores dealing in hand-painted Herend porcelain plates and other souvenirs of the kind snapped up by foreign tourists from the west, but what western visitor would want to buy expensive intimate garments in Budapest when a far wider selection was available in Vienna just a few hours' drive away?

A lady who has just embarked on a glamorous affair with a mysterious spy, that's who, she said to herself, and giggled aloud. She paused to admire a heavily embroidered evening jacket in a window a few yards further on, and then realised that she had company. As a small hand tugged at her sleeve she caught sight of two reflections beside her own in the glass.

"Missis! Give me dollar!" muttered a very familiar voice.

Emma smiled down at Emma and Sandor. "For goodness sake, have you two followed me here all the way from Debrecen?"

To her surprise Agnes violently shook her dirty little head. "You don' know us, Missis," she whispered, and then raised her voice again into her practised beggar's whine. "Gimme dollar-deutschmark-forints, lady!"

It took Emma a moment to catch on, but then she entered into the role Agnes seemed to be prescribing for her and rummaged in her bag, mouthing cliches, while Sandor gazed up at her with his liquid brown eyes and Agnes spoke to her with solemn urgency.

"Mister get my note okay?"

"Yes. I think so, but I don't know what you said in it." Then, more loudly for public consumption, "I can't find any dollars. Here's some Hungarian money . . ."

"You tell him to go Hortobagy like I said. Famous bridge there. STINGY BASTARD!" Agnes added at the top of her voice as she and Sandor skipped off at the approach of a policeman in uniform, who warned Emma in hesitant English not to give money to beggar children. "They pick pocket," he explained helpfully.

"Oh gosh, I didn't realise that. Thank you very much," Emma said contritely, and the policeman saluted her with an indulgent smile. You bet they do, but that's not the half of it, Emma added contentedly to herself as she resumed her stroll.

Chapter Nineteen

"Hortobagy? What about Hortobagy?"

"That's what it said in this note I'm talking about. I saw it in his letter box when I arrived for work this morning. Took it upstairs with me, but I copied it first. Here."

Rozsika thrust a scrap of paper at the man to whom she routinely reported about once a week. In her own opinion she hardly ever had anything juicy to pass on: descriptions of Lazenby's occasional luncheon guests, vague accounts of overheard conversations at table – here Rozsika, whose comprehension of idiomatic spoken English wasn't really up to much, let her creative imagination take over – and, by way of material intelligence, the torn-up invitation cards and crumpled envelopes which were all that Lazenby left in his waste-paper basket. Having a shrewd idea where such ephemera ended up, he had toyed with the idea of planting misinformation just for the fun of it, but much as he had come to admire the black Hungarian sense of humour, he had decided in favour of seemly prudence.

Gabor Foldes, forty-three, was ostensibly a member of the managerial staff of the Hungarian State Domestic Employment Agency and in reality a very minor security official. He was thin and prematurely bald, and an anxious smile settled over his features when they were in repose. He looked unhappily at Rozsika as he took the paper.

"That's in my writing, what you've got there, remember," she said. "I want to make that clear." Rozsika was already beginning to think she was showing an excess of zeal, and to have misgivings. It would never do if the powers that be were to get hold of the idea that she was the person calling herself Agnes for the purpose of making furtive assignations with Lazenby.

"I put down exactly what it said in the note while I was still downstairs. I mean, before I took it up and gave it to him." She thought of adding that she found him having breakfast in the company of a young female professor from Debrecen, with whom he had obviously passed an enjoyable night. She didn't do so, though, partly because it was Saturday and she was anxious to get home, but mainly because she considered that she had already done more than enough that month to earn the meagre supplement to her pay that she received from the AVH.

Foldes studied Rozsika's transcript with a sinking feeling. He had no idea what the message might mean, but had an uneasy feeling that he would be required to explain it, or at least suggest a plausible hypothesis to account for it. There was of course an alternative to passing the note upwards to his own superior: he could simply lose it. The snag there that was that it had been a long time since he had been in a position to pass on a really tasty morsel; and rightly handled, this enigmatic message might lead to a pat on the back from on high. He therefore decided to pull himself together, cleared his throat portentously and nodded in a meaning way.

"You did well, Comrade. Quick thinking. If this means what I think it might, I shall recommend some official recognition of your efforts."

Rozsika blushed. "That would be nice. Thank you." She shuffled her feet. "What I'd really like," she added shyly after a moment or two, "is one of those electric mixers."

"What, I wonder, is special about Hortobagy?" asked the KGB Deputy Resident.

"It's where the pancakes come from," a young, darkly

handsome lieutenant from the Military Attaché's office put in helpfully, earning himself a withering look from Colonel Pavel Galitsin, whose cousin Major Vishinski had after all set the whole business moving and who therefore felt a proprietary interest in seeing it come to a satisfactory conclusion. The Colonel spoke up in a no-nonsense military manner, referring to a clipboard he had before him.

"Hortobagy is the name given to a large area of the Great Hungarian Plain or *puszta*, some 100,000 hectares in extent and designated as a national park about ten years ago. It is also the name of a small village which lies approximately forty kilometres west of the city of Debrecen and is the main point of tourist access to the national park. The area is famous for its so-called Great Fish Pond – which takes bird-watchers best part of a day to walk round – and its rare plant and animal species. These include longhorn cattle, *racka* sheep, wild horses and prairie dogs – "

"– And the pancakes we've heard about already, and which are particularly good at Gundel's Restaurant here in Budapest. Thank you, Colonel. Very informative, but what I was going to go on to ask is where it might be possible to conceal a large refrigerated truck in the vicinity. I convened this meeting in a hurry because information was received by the AVH earlier this afternoon to the effect that the interesting Mr Benjamin Lazenby of the British Embassy has been summoned to Hortobagy tomorrow morning at eleven by somebody using the code name 'Agnes', presumably in connection with the truck I referred to a moment ago." She crossed her elegantly clad legs and glanced down to admire her ankles.

"That is what the Hungarians think, anyway, because as soon as they heard about the message to Lazenby, the police were instructed to carry out an immediate search in and around Hortobagy village for the Bulgarian truck that the Institute of Cultural Relations mislaid and are very anxious to find. One of two similar vehicles, it is said to contain about half the paintings comprising an exhibition sent by the British under the terms of the Anglo-Hungarian Cultural Agreement, and which were transported from Bucharest by road. The other half are in safe custody at the National Fine Art Gallery. You may well wonder, as I do myself, why Bulgarian vehicles were used."

Svetlana Ivanova looked at her watch, a genuine Cartier. "But that is by the way. It is now nearly six-thirty, getting dark, and I have not heard that the police search has been successful. I might mention that Mr Lazenby himself seems to be relatively unconcerned about the whereabouts of his valuable oil paintings. He arrived back in Budapest yesterday, and devoted his evening and much of the night to entertaining and being entertained by a woman friend. Moreover, I understand that today he has been instrumental in wrecking an AVH car and putting its driver in hospital with a broken leg. One can't help admiring his stamina. So if he does indeed go to Hortobagy tomorrow morning I think it would be to our advantage to keep an eye on him." She looked at each of the others in turn. "Now, Comrades, where in that extensive area might he keep an unobtrusive rendezvous at eleven in the morning?"

There followed a protracted silence, broken at last by the lieutenant, who wanted very much to redeem himself. "Er, may I suggest Mata? It's just a hamlet really, quite near the famous Nine-Arch Bridge. But several times every day at this time of the year groups of up to twenty tourists are driven from there in horse-drawn covered wagons on a two-hour trip to see the sheep and cattle the Comrade Colonel was talking about. And there are, well, sort of stunts. Trick riding and so on."

"Hm. It sounds as if you've sampled this treat yourself, Lieutenant. Lots of westerners among the tourists?"

"Yes." The young officer rather mumbled the words that followed. "It's quite expensive, you see. Several hundred forints."

Svetlana Ivanova cupped her ear and leaned forward ostentatiously. "Is it indeed? Well, Colonel, even if I've heard him aright, it's not for me to enquire how the lieutenant could afford such a treat. Nevertheless, I'm much obliged to him for his useful suggestion. It sounds the most likely spot in the Hortobagy area for a meet, and I shall see that one or more of my staff are at this Mata place in the morning. I may very well go myself. You may wish to arrange a discreet Soviet Army presence also, since it was of course an army officer who first drew our attention to this whole affair."

Colonel Galitsin nodded curtly and tucked his clipboard under his arm, half-rising. "If there is nothing further, Comrade?"

"No, this has been a useful meeting from my point of view. Thank you for sparing time for it. And thank *you*, Lieutenant." The Deputy Resident flashed a brilliant smile at the young man as he left the room in his master's wake.

Alone again, she made a mental note to put in a good word for the lieutenant with the Military Attaché himself. It didn't matter what poor old Colonel Galitsin thought. He had a pedestrian mind, unlike his boss the General and the lieutenant. Who was, incidentally, both charming and personable as well as quick-witted.

Svetlana Ivanova sighed, moistened her lips with the tip of her tongue and fondled her solid silver Cross ballpoint pen. Then she abruptly put it aside, slightly ashamed of fantasising when there were puzzles to be thought about. The Hungarian security service's almost embarrassing eagerness to please was a source of general amusement throughout the KGB Residency. The people at large might make darkly humorous anti-Soviet remarks, but their spooks at least knew on which side their bread was buttered.

That being so, it was significant that the AVH had not volunteered an explanation of their own interest, as distinct from that of the KKI, in this wretched lorry. And why had they arrested the Finnish journalist who was in the company of Lazenby at the Art Gallery earlier? It was a good thing that one of the attendants there was a KGB source, or Svetlana Ivanova might never have known about that curious ingredient in the story that seemed to be unfolding.

By the end of the afternoon Lazenby had done what he could for Gosta, who had in spite of her distress had to try hard to keep a straight face when she saw the AVH driver sprawling on the ground in agony, groaning oaths while the unoccupied car gathered speed and her captors watched with dismay as it crashed into a concrete bollard with a clang of buckling metal.

It occurred to Lazenby that he might take advantage of the confusion and seize the opportunity to spirit Gosta away in a taxi, but he realised almost at once that it would be a madly reckless course of action which would do neither of them any good. Standing there indecisively, he saw Gosta gesture to him with her hand, waving him away; so with an unhappy shrug he made his own escape.

He found a taxi and went straight to the Finnish Embassy, identified himself and asked to speak urgently and in confidence to a member of the consular staff. He was admitted without delay, and seen by a vice-consul, whose sardonically cool expression was transformed into one of eager attention when Lazenby mentioned the name of Gosta Lundin and explained that he had made her acquaintance recently in Bucharest. Lazenby then reported soberly that he had, quite by chance, encountered Ms Lundin at the Art Museum that morning and had a short social conversation with her which was rudely interrupted by her apprehension by two presumed agents of the Hungarian security service. He went on to say that he had tried unsuccessfully to intervene, whereupon Ms Lundin had requested him to inform her Embassy.

"She asked me to contact Reuters news agency too, but I think it might be preferable if your own press attache were to do that."

"This is very disturbing news, Mr Lazenby. I will make official enquiries at once, and advise Reuters after I get a reaction from the Hungarian authorities. It's very good of you to have come forward in this way."

"It's the least I could do. You do understand that I'm acting in my private capacity, as a personal acquaintance of Gosta Lundin, and not on behalf of the British Embassy."

"Of course. It would be quite inappropriate for your Embassy to be involved in such a matter."

Lazenby returned to his own office after that, and tried to behave as if he had nothing special on his mind. He passed the Ambassador in the corridor and, when asked when he was off to Sofia, replied with forced nonchalance that it was Bucharest, not Sofia, that he had in fact just returned and that everything had gone very well. Then, when Joanna looked in to apologise again for "inflicting" Emma on him, he did his best to imply that he bore such intrusions, however tiresome, with philosophical resignation. Joanna was clearly keen to know what had been on Emma's mind, but Lazenby fobbed her off by pretending not to understand, and telling her that he was, alas, stuck with Emma until the next day.

In between times he dealt with a few papers, brooded about Gosta, and occasionally studied the note purporting to be from Agnes. What was it Gosta had said when it became clear that the two goons were going to take her away? Something to the effect that, if there were any messages – and she had stressed that word – she wanted him to act on them. Well, he'd behaved pretty contemptibly when she appealed for his help in Romania, and he could at least try to make amends by putting himself out this time. Lazenby took the piece of paper from his wallet and looked at it yet again. Hortobagy. Tomorrow, eleven o'clock.

He rubbed his eyes wearily. It was undoubtedly a message, and equally certainly, Gosta had employed the gipsy children in a minor role in what she had as good as admitted was an elaborate deception. So she might easily use them again, as messengers this time. But the note had been put into his letter box *before* her arrest; and in any case, since she was in Budapest there were far simpler ways for her to get in touch with him than that. So who was the message from? What the *hell* was going on?

The day had begun so well, too, with him looking forward keenly to a second exciting night with Emma, who was, it suddenly occurred to him as he glanced at his watch, even now probably making her way demurely to Gerbaud's round the corner to meet him. Stifling an ungallant groan, he gathered up the papers on his desk to take them down to Registry, looked round his office to make sure he hadn't forgotten anything, and went out, locking the door behind him. At least he'd made sure that Emma hadn't seen the note . . .

Emma Jarvis was not only waiting for him when he arrived at Gerbaud's five minutes late, but had achieved the almost impossible in the perpetually crowded cafe in securing a table for two and defending the vacant seat against all comers. Her eyes were sparkling and she looked so pleased to see him that he surprised himself by bending over her and kissing her warmly and at some length.

"Down, boy," she gasped happily, while recovering her breath. "I'm glad to see you too. I hope you've had an interesting day – mine was absolutely fascinating. Guess who I met?" She looked around and then lowered her voice in a stagily conspiratorial manner. "Agnes and Sandor! And Agnes gave me a message for you . . ."

Chapter Twenty

"For Christ's sake shut up, Emma!"

Startled by the rapidity with which Lazenby's expression darkened and offended by the tone of his voice, Emma blinked at him, temporarily speechless, while Lazenby irritably signalled to a passing waitress and snapped an order for two coffees. Then she gave vent to her own displeasure at being addressed so curtly.

"Actually," she remarked icily, "and had you consulted me, I would have said I'd quite like one of those peaches made out of marzipan."

"Another time." Lazenby glanced round nervously. "This is no place to talk." He drummed his fingers impatiently on the table.

"For goodness sake, Ben! Anybody would think I'd said something outrageous! All I wanted to tell you – "

"Save it. Here comes our coffee."

Lazenby paid for the coffee on delivery, and gulped his own at speed, glaring at Emma while she mutinously took her time over hers. The moment she finally put her cup down he stood.

"Come on, then. The car's round the corner."

Much offended, Emma trailed out after him, then after walking a few yards while thinking hard, stopped short and confronted him. "Look, I'm sorry."

"It's all right."

Emma was by now repenting her prickliness. She reminded herself that while Lazenby in his role as the

British Cultural Attaché might be expected to display an easy mastery of the social graces – and had indeed done so in Debrecen – she'd forgotten for the moment that even though they had become lovers he was after all a secret agent, living dangerously and with every right to warn her peremptorily to hold her tongue when she was about to be indiscreet.

"No, you were right to choke me off. It was stupid of me to blurt that out in there. I'm afraid I've got a lot to learn about this business."

"What business?"

Emma opened her mouth to tell him to come off it, then closed it again virtuously and shook her head. Lazenby shrugged, clearly still exasperated. "Well, what about Agnes and Sandor? Where did you see them? You can tell me now." He began to walk on, taking a roundabout route to where his car was parked so as to secure more time before they would have to watch their words again.

"Not far from here. In the smart shopping street, Vaci Utca, isn't it?"

While a chastened Emma went on to describe her encounter with the two children, Lazenby listened attentively and concluded that his plan to keep her in ignorance of the contents of the note Rozsika had handed him was utterly confounded. Then it occurred to him that her account lacked something.

"Could you repeat the precise words Agnes used?"

"Well, not word for word exactly, but it was something like 'tell him to go Hortobagy like I said'. Then she mentioned a famous bridge there."

"Just Hortobagy . . . and a famous bridge. Nothing else."

"No. Well, apart from warning me not to say anything to indicate that I knew them."

"I see." Even when reporting what Agnes had said for a second time, Emma hadn't mentioned the key words "tomorrow" or "11 hours". She had shown already that she was capable of holding things back, but it seemed at least possible, even probable, that she had faithfully passed on the message which Agnes had given her. So even now he might not need to come completely clean with her.

Having to watch Gosta being taken away that morning had been a sobering experience, and not the least of its consequences was that he now regretted the greed for more lovemaking with Emma that had made him so eager to agree when she invited herself to stay at his house for a second night. The prospect of devoting hours to self-indulgence while knowing that Gosta Lundin was in the hands of the AVH had during the course of the day begun to seem more and more ignoble, and it now began to look as if there might be a way out.

Quite apart from his own desire to salvage some self-respect by helping Gosta, he ought to think about Emma's position, and avoid embroiling her even more in what seemed to be developing into a thoroughly messy business. He rubbed his forehead as he tried to assess the risk of what he was inclined to say next, and Emma looked up at him with tender concern. "You'll have to go to Hortobagy, obviously."

"Well, I suppose so. Though I can't imagine what I can expect to find there."

"I don't expect you to tell me, Ben," Emma said wistfully, and then suddenly recalled a phrase she had come across in John Le Carré. "I realise it's probably all on a 'need to know' basis."

Lazenby was touched, and came to a decision. Emma would be disappointed, but if he were to soften the blow . . . he came to a halt, turned to her and took both her hands in his. "Well, you're right, but there is something important I see no reason not to tell you. You remember the name Gosta Lundin? The journalist from Finland?"

"Yes, of course. She gave the tape to Agnes."

"Yes. Well, I'm afraid she was picked up and taken away by the Hungarian security police today."

Emma experienced a brief moment of relief which she at once realised was unworthy. Though Ben had denied that Gosta was his lady friend, she had retained some doubts on the subject. "Oh God, how dreadful!"

"Yes. Every effort's being made to secure her release, but, listen Emma, I don't know how to break this to you, but I'm afraid I'm going to have to, er, postpone our date and drive you back to Debrecen tonight." He looked at his watch and surreptitiously crossed his fingers.

"It's a little after half-past five now, and I'm due at Hortobagy at eleven. It's very near Debrecen, you know. So why don't we go to the house and pick up your things, then I'll drive you straight home. It's not much over a hundred and twenty miles, and a good fast road; much quicker than the train, and I'll be able to enjoy your company on the way. I can drop you at your flat well before ten, and then go on to Hortobagy. It's only about twenty miles . . ."

Well, the die was cast. He tried to read Emma's expression. It was crestfallen, but she nodded sadly, and seemingly without surprise; and she made no attempt to persuade him to allow her to go with him to Hortobagy. Lazenby breathed again.

"Of course, Ben. Whatever you think best. First things first, and I can understand you won't want me around to distract you. There'll be other times, I hope."

"Of *course* there will, dearest Emma. Believe me, I'm horribly disappointed, and . . . well, I want to apologise for snapping at you earlier. I do have rather a lot on my mind."

During the ten-minute drive across the Danube and up to the house Lazenby was more than reassured that he had succeeded in deceiving her, at the self-inflicted cost to himself of an exhausting drive. For Emma lightened the mood dramatically, by describing her sighting of the haggard, scruffy and woebegone Dracula in such vivid terms that her account brought Lazenby close to hysteria. He realised that he was in a peculiar, hopped-up condition and that he ought to calm down, but it was no use. After nearly colliding with a lamppost he stopped to wipe the tears of laughter from his eyes, and then managed to reach the house without accident; but it had been a near thing.

Comrade Nagy had arrived back at the Institute of Cultural Relations from Szolnok an hour or so earlier, bearing the news that a badly hung over Ivan, whose name was in fact Teodor Grobkov, had stuck to the story he had told the Szolnok police after sobering up. This was to the effect that he had been diverted from the highway into a minor road a short distance beyond Kecskemet by a man dressed in what he took to be police uniform. Once out of sight of the main Budapest road he had found his way blocked by a rattletrap van, and on climbing down from his cab to investigate he was rushed and seized by about half a dozen shabbily dressed men who looked to him like gipsies. Two of their number took his place in the air-conditioned truck, while the others tied his wrists behind his back and bundled him into the van. Inside, one of them held his head and pinched his nostrils while another poured a quantity of plum liquor into his open mouth. Then the van got under way, and he heard his own lorry being driven along behind. By the sound of it, the man at the wheel knew how to handle it, Grobkov added with reluctant respect.

The not entirely disagreeable torture by alcohol was repeated every few minutes, until the Bulgarian captive was in a stupefied state. He couldn't remember when or where his own vehicle parted company with the van, and had only the haziest recollection of being dumped in the town of Szolnok, by which time his wrists had been freed. No, his abductors hadn't spoken to each other during the period he was still *compos mentis*, nor had they answered him when he protested, which he had done vigorously in both his native Bulgarian and in Russian. And he'd had enough of craziness of one sort and another and wanted to be taken to his Embassy, please.

"I wonder if the Bulgarian Embassy has in fact been informed?" Szekacs asked.

"Search me. They're bringing him here to Pest, to central police headquarters, and I don't much care what they decide to do with him. It's the fucking truck I'm interested in. Among other things." Szekacs winced at the crudity of his language, but then he seemed to have spent much of the past twenty-four hours wincing.

"Crafty buggers, though, you have to admit," Nagy went on in a ruminative way. "Dumping him outside a Grade Four stand-up bar full of other drunks. I should think it was quite a while before anybody even noticed him. Gave them plenty of time to make a clean getaway. Anyway, got another bit of news for you: the Englishman's up to something."

Before turning up in Szekacs's office, Nagy had checked in to his controller at AVH headquarters, who had graciously told him about Rozsika's information, just received there. Nagy took sadistic pleasure in passing it on to Szekacs, who by that time looked like a zombie and merely gaped dully.

"Hortobagy. Got it? Eleven tomorrow morning. Should be interesting, so I've decided we'll go too. Be ready to leave from here about seven." Nagy's summary order spurred Szekacs to feeble protest, which was ruthlessly overridden. Nagy seemed to be thriving on all the excitement, and no longer troubled even to go through the motions of behaving as a mere driver. He ended the one-sided discussion by ordering Szekacs to go home and get some sleep, and then bustled out of the room.

Left to himself again, Viktor Szekacs tasted the bitter dregs of humiliation at the hands of the very man whose pigheaded obtuseness had brought his orderly world tumbling about his ears. He glumly savoured the thought of killing Comrade Nagy, and even ran through possible murder methods in his imagination, before concluding sadly that his own condition, both physically and mentally, was so debilitated that any such course of action was out of the question for the time being. So he did as he was bidden, went home and, at about the time Lazenby and Emma were setting out for Debrecen, collapsed into a sleep more profound than any he could remember experiencing for many years.

Chapter Twenty-One

"Well, it is Saturday evening, after all. People are getting away from Budapest for the weekend, I suppose. You'd be surprised how many people own holiday shacks. But most of those are around Lake Balaton, and we're heading in the opposite direction. I think we'll be okay."

Lazenby had driven down the hill from his house and through the monumental Vienna Gate that marked the boundary of the old walled Castle Hill of Buda, only to find the main road choked with traffic. He was already wondering if it had been such a good idea after all to talk Emma into going back, but having told her that his mysterious rendezvous at Hortobagy was set for twelve hours earlier than Agnes had specified in her note, he was stuck with the consequences.

In the event his show of optimism about the traffic conditions ahead of them proved to be justified, and after a tricky quarter of an hour they were out of the centre and making good time along the road to Szolnok and Debrecen. A few minutes later they were passing the airport on their left and well on their way.

He had washed his face while Emma was gathering up her belongings, and made himself calm down, aware that he had reacted with nervously excessive hilarity to the picture of Dracula she had so comically evoked. Viktor Szekacs was very teasable, but not to be written off as simply a figure of fun; and he represented politically powerful interests. Belatedly Lazenby realised that he wasn't in ideal shape to face a round trip to Debrecen which would probably get him back to his house in the small hours. He'd be able to snatch no more than a few hours of sleep before having to make an early start on another long and worrying drive, into the unknown at Hortobagy, at the behest of a scruffy gipsy child. Last night with Emma had been exhilarating indeed, but demanding, and he wondered seriously whether he would be able to keep awake at the wheel for the next six or seven hours. He took a deep breath and blew the air out of his pursed lips noisily.

As Emma cast him a quizzical look, he smiled. "Talk to me, please. Otherwise I'm afraid I might fall asleep."

"Really? I should have thought you'd be much too excited for that, heading for a clandestine meeting on the strength of a secret message."

He shook his head resignedly. "I'm a NATO diplomat, Emma, and this car has a distinctive number plate. By now the authorities will have been notified that I'm leaving Budapest in a south-easterly direction with a woman passenger. And since they certainly know you stayed at my house last night, they'll infer quite correctly that I'm driving you back to Debrecen."

He forbore to add that, to make assurance doubly sure, he had taken the opportunity while Emma was in the bathroom to make a quick telephone call to Joanna Crockett who was fortunately at home, to tell her that he was about to do just that. He asked her to let the night duty officer know that he'd be out of town for a few hours. It turned out that Joanna was herself on duty that night, so Lazenby put down the phone in the virtual certainty that her own telephone bug would have been activated.

Emma gazed at him, appalled. "But how on earth . . . I mean, only Joanna Crockett knows I stayed with you, surely?"

"Joanna and a lot of other people."

"But how?"

"I did warn you my house is bugged."

"But . . . surely they don't, well, I mean . . ."

Lazenby shook his head and smiled with gloomy relish. Emma Jarvis had been enjoying playing spies, but the time had come to enlighten her about some of the less glamorous aspects of the security business.

"I'm not important enough to rate twenty-four hour surveillance, but they're in a position to listen in on me whenever it suits them. One gets used to the idea after a while."

"The very thought makes me shudder. How can you bear it?"

"Oh, come on. They keep an eye on you too, to a lesser extent. You're a foreigner being paid out of Hungarian public funds, after all. Your nice Professor Horvath gave you permission to come to Budapest, so that's fine, but when you arrived you visited the Embassy. Even if the Hungarian security guard on duty outside didn't log you going in, he'll certainly have reported that you left again with Joanna. Who took you first to her place and then brought you to mine. And remember we were having breakfast when Rozsika turned up, and I introduced you."

"Are you telling me that your cleaning lady is – "

"An informer? Almost certainly."

"Oh, my God!" Emma relapsed into a stunned silence for a short time, and out of the corner of his eye he saw her flush and raise a hand to her throat. When she next spoke the pitch of her voice had risen to a near-squeak. "So it's quite likely that someone was *listening* when I, while we – "

"Quite likely, I'm afraid. Sorry. Do you mind?"

"Well, not exactly, I suppose, but it's a rather devastating thought all the same."

"Oh, I don't know. Anyone who's ever had a room in

a university hall of residence has heard the twanging of bedsprings etcetera through the wall."

Another short silence, then: "That woman, Rosie something – "

"Rozsika."

"She brought that note upstairs, Ben! She'd had time to read it first!"

"Yes, I'd thought of that."

"So perhaps they *know* you're going to Hortobagy tonight."

Lazenby shrugged. He was quite sure they knew he was going to Hortobagy, not that night but the next day, and was apprehensive about the consequences for himself. Yet the only alternative was the contemptible one of disregarding Gosta's appeal. There was probably little enough he could do to help the Romanian gipsies, but Gosta seemed to think he had a part to play. He thought of Agnes, that proud, perky little girl; and of her younger brother's manifest faith in and devotion to her, and blinked away the tears that welled up in his eyes. He had to do what he could for the poor little buggers and those who trusted and relied on them. When Emma spoke next it was as if she had read his mind.

"Ben, about that tape recording. What's on it that makes it so important?"

"I haven't listened to it, and that's the truth."

"Nor have I, though obviously I could have done. But that wasn't what I asked you."

Lazenby thought hard before deciding that he owed it to Emma to be a little more forthcoming. She had, after all, been in possession of the tape herself for a day. "No, I know it wasn't. The simple answer is that Gosta Lundin considers it important, and although I hardly know her, I respect her. And presumably others think it important, since she's now been arrested."

"Well, I'm not going to ask you how you discovered

that, obviously. But you might at least give me some idea why Agnes and Sandor are still mixed up in this whole business. When they handed the tape over to me that ought to have been the end of it as far as they're concerned."

"I can only pass on the gist of what Gosta told me. She described the recording as being of the voice of . . . a prominent politician, talking in recklessly indiscreet terms about a policy that if brought into effect would have very serious consequences for all gipsies. I think Gosta Lundin hopes to expose him and put a huge spanner in the works. I don't suppose for one moment that Agnes and Sandor know anything about what's on the tape. They're young children, after all, but because they're brave and resourceful, their people are using them as messengers. Please don't ask me to say any more. I shouldn't really have told you that much."

"Thank you anyway. I'm sorry I've been so naive. The tape is in a safe place now, isn't it?"

"Yes."

They were nearing Szolnok, and Lazenby checked his fuel gauge. The needle was dangerously close to the red warning area, and filling stations where one could buy the premium grade the Rover needed were few and far between. Szolnok was a big enough place to boast one.

"Keep an eye open for a garage, would you. We need petrol."

There wasn't anywhere on the western outskirts, and Lazenby drove cautiously through the centre of the city, with mounting anxiety, followed by relief when he saw an illuminated sign, a forecourt showing signs of life and, best of all, a pump for superior grade petrol. He pulled in beside it, and a man in stained overalls approached, having pointedly scrutinised the blue number plate.

"We're not authorised to sell duty-free," he announced

with glum satisfaction. Just in time Lazenby spotted the Party membership badge pinned to his overalls.

"No matter, Comrade. I don't approve of diplomatic privileges anyway. The price ordinary workers pay is good enough for me. Will you fill her up, please?"

Emma didn't understand Lazenby's Hungarian, but she sensed that the man needed some encouragement to be helpful, and bestowed a dazzling smile on him, upon which he very slowly moved towards the pump, looking slightly nonplussed. Lazenby quickly got out, keys at the ready, and unlocked and removed the cap to the petrol tank.

Still obviously none too sure he wanted to, the garage man nevertheless inserted the nozzle and after a final brief hesitation pulled the trigger. "This is an English car," he said. "You English?"

"Yes, that's right."

"Capitalist."

"Well, not personally, Comrade. I'm a worker like you." Lazenby had a couple of thousand pounds in the Abbey National, but considered that this hardly turned him into a rentier. The attendant smiled sourly.

"You? Don't make me laugh. A diplomat, with a fancy car like this? That your wife?"

"No, she's a professor at Debrecen University. I'm driving her home."

"You called me Comrade."

"Of course. I regard all the Hungarian people as my comrades. Some of my best friends are Party members like you."

"Name one."

"Ivan Boldizsar of the Writers' Union," Lazenby said promptly, and hoped to be forgiven. By then the tank was full, and he stopped caring. "And a man called Viktor Szekacs," he added. A final test awaited him, though.

"If this *had* been a duty-free garage, you'd have had to pay in hard currency."

"Yes, I know." Something about the man's expression bothered Lazenby. Was he or wasn't he on the fiddle? If he were to offer sterling instead of Hungarian forints to a Party member, what would happen? Would it be accepted gratefully, or would he be denounced for attempting to corrupt a decent worker? He drew out his wallet slowly, agonising over what could be quite an important decision, then chanced his arm.

"Oh, damn!" he said in English, then went on in Hungarian. "I've just realised I don't have enough forints on me. Plenty of English money, but . . . just a minute, I'll see if my passenger can help me out – "

"No need to bother her. In the circumstances, I don't mind taking English money. I won't be able to give you any change, though."

Reassured but pretending to be still dubious, Lazenby took out a five-pound note, and the man reached for it eagerly. "You're sure it's all right, Comrade? Well, thank you."

"That'll be fine. Thank *you*, Comrade. Have a good trip." The garage man watched until the tail lights of the Rover were out of sight. He thought Lazenby was all right, really, in spite of being a capitalist.

About half an hour later Lazenby blinked, braked hard and brought the Rover to a halt with a screech of its tyres. Emma had dozed off and woke with a start. "What on earth . . . is something wrong?"

"No, it's okay. Some idiot just came out of a side lane driving a horse and cart of all things. No lights, needless to say." He sat there shaking his head in exasperation as the man aboard the cart unconcernedly directed the plodding horse straight across the main road and into another unmarked track leading off the other side. They both watched the cart disappear into the darkness.

"Damn good job there's nothing coming the other

way," Lazenby said, then peered fixedly into the rear-view mirror. "Hang *on* . . ." Then he put the car into reverse and backed up about two hundred yards. "I could have sworn . . ." he went on muttering, more or less to himself.

"What is it, Ben?"

"Just a minute. I've got to check this. For a moment I thought I saw . . ."

"Saw *what*, for goodness sake?"

Lazenby stopped the car and doused the lights, then switched off the ignition. "Wait in the car," he said, ignoring Emma's question. "I'll be back in a minute or two."

It was in a lean-to shed beside the road in what looked like open country, in that the nearest buildings in sight were at least a quarter of a mile away, and no lights were visible. Lazenby waited with his eyes closed for a good ten seconds, and looked again. It wasn't a particularly dark night, and the lettering on the side was clearly legible. Moreover, the air conditioning machinery was rumbling away as it had done throughout the night in Arad.

Lazenby could hardly believe his eyes. What in the world was the missing Bulgarian lorry doing here of all places?

Chapter Twenty-Two

His heart pounding, Lazenby approached the vehicle and surveyed it, going first to its rear. Yes, it really was Ivan's: the Romanian government customs seals were intact. He then walked round to the front. In the gloom and at close quarters the massive flank looked forbidding, and when he reached the separate cab he saw that its window was far too high for him to look inside. He noticed a metal bracket that provided the lowest foothold, and the recess above it that served as the second step up, and saw that there was a hand grip within his reach.

As quietly as possible he put his right foot in the bracket, grasped the hand grip and hauled himself off the ground, trying to find the recess with his left foot. After a few fumbled attempts he succeeded and as he clung there, was able to peer through the window. He fully expected to see Ivan stretched out across the seats: asleep or drunk, he knew not what, but the three seats were unoccupied. Lazenby raised himself a little more so that he could see the floor, but no, Ivan hadn't bedded down there either.

His legs were aching and he was giving himself a crick in his neck, but he hung there indecisively for nearly a minute longer before groping for the handle of the door and trying it. It yielded at once, and Lazenby awkwardly swung himself into the cab, which he was then able to confirm he had to himself.

The rumble of the air conditioning machinery was less noticeable inside, and Lazenby gratefully sat in the driver's seat and eased his protesting leg muscles while taking stock. The ignition key was in place and the cab comfortably warm; suggesting that Ivan had stopped so that he could respond to a call of nature. But that explanation had nothing to do with the basic question, which was where the hell he thought he was going anyway. There were other considerations. If Ivan simply needed to get out for a pee, surely he'd do it beside the truck? And challenge anybody who approached out of nowhere and clamber in after taking a careful look around? And most puzzling, why park the juggernaut so carefully in this lean-to, where it was partially concealed?

After pondering for a while, Lazenby remembered that he had left Emma on her own in the Rover, and that she would be wondering what had become of him. He opened the door again and looked down at the ground, which seemed a long way away, and stretched out a foot, lodging the heel of his shoe in the foothold. Then he jumped, stumbling badly before regaining his balance, and reached up to close the door.

Returning to his own car, he slid into his own seat and began to apologise to Emma. "I'm sorry to have been so long, but it's the most extraordinary thing. There's a lorry over there, and I don't know what to do about it."

"I was getting nervous, but that's okay. Why do you need to do anything about it?"

"Because it's got about half a million pounds worth of paintings inside, that's why. And it went missing yesterday afternoon."

"*What* did you say?"

"It's half of the exhibition I was supposed to escort from Bucharest. And through my own bloody stupidity and negligence I mislaid it."

"But didn't think to mention it to me. And now you've found it again. How nice."

Disregarding Emma's heavy sarcasm, Lazenby started

the Rover and backed it further until it was directly alongside the cab of the truck. If and when Ivan did deign to put in an appearance, he had no intention of allowing him to drive it off into the night. Meantime he had some intensive thinking to do and some difficult decisions to take.

He now strongly suspected that this was not the million-to-one coincidence that he had originally supposed. Somebody had placed the truck there for him to find, and the man with the horse and cart must have been part of the arrangement, deliberately timing his emergence from the narrow, unmade side lane and into their path, at considerable risk to himself, his horse and his cart. If Lazenby hadn't been obliged to brake so violently, the odds were that he'd have driven straight past Ivan's truck and on to Debrecen without ever spotting it.

What on earth was he to do? Wait for a while, of course, to see if Ivan or anybody else returned to the lorry. While waiting, scout around again and shout a bit. But if nobody came? In that event, the most straightforward course of action for a more or less law-abiding diplomat would be to switch on his hazard warning lights, get the red triangle sign out of the boot, place it in the road behind the car and wait for the first cooperative driver to stop. Then request him politely to inform the police as soon as he could reach a telephone.

On the other hand, bringing in the police would entail all the consequences Lazenby had thought of and spelt out to the cringing Szekacs outside the museum the previous evening. And another thing. If he was right about the man with the horse and cart, this whole stagey business could be interpreted as a message from the gipsies, though if that were the case its meaning was unfathomable. The fellow who'd risked his neck to bring the Rover screeching to a halt in the middle of nowhere could very well be a gipsy himself. But how could Agnes and Sandor's controllers possibly have known he'd be coming, when it wasn't much more than a couple of hours ago that he'd decided more or less on the spur of the moment to drive Emma back to Debrecen that evening?

On the other hand, he had done his best to make sure that the AVH spooks knew of his intention. It could be that the Hungarian authorities had found and taken possession of the truck much sooner. They clearly knew that Gosta was up to something, and his encounter with her at the gallery that morning, though innocent enough as far as Lazenby was concerned, would have convinced them that he was her accomplice. Especially when they thought about what had happened to their man outside and to one of their cars.

They probably knew about the tape, and suspected that Gosta might have concealed it aboard the lorry. Lazenby now knew that the one he had hidden in the Birtwistle box in his filing cabinet was a decoy. So perhaps the AVH had by now actually found the original. In which case they could be stringing him along. As well as Szekacs, in that event, for he had seen him with his own eyes the previous afternoon, and there was no doubt that he was a genuinely worried man. And Emma had spotted him that very morning looking even more worried.

"Ben. Are you going to enlighten me, or do you propose to sit there like a stuffed dummy all evening?"

"What? Oh. Look, I'm sorry. My head's spinning, and I honestly don't know where I am."

"I can tell you that much, at least. While you were communing with your lorry I looked at the map, and I think we're near a village called Kenderes. About two-thirds of the way to Debrecen. And frankly I don't care what you decide, but I'd be obliged if you'd make up your mind soon."

"I know you're fed up and I don't blame you, but you're part of the problem, you see."

"Thanks very much, I'm sure," Emma said tartly.

"No, let me try to explain before you fly off the handle. Through no fault of your own, you've discovered a great deal more than is good for you – "

"Don't patronise me, Ben."

"Emma, please just *listen* for a minute. You've become involved in what could be a very dangerous business for you. Much more so than for me. I've been sticking my neck out, but as a diplomat I'm personally more or less fireproof. In the old days none of the Soviet bloc governments cared tuppence about the niceties, but the Hungarians at least are scrupulous about diplomatic immunity now. They won't throw me in jail come what may. The worst that can happen to me is that I'll be declared *persona non grata* and my Ambassador will send me back to London with my tail between my legs. You, on the other hand, are subject in every way to Hungarian law. You could be arrested – as Gosta Lundin has been – and imprisoned if you upset the authorities."

"But I haven't done anything wrong, Ben. Professor Horvath gave me permission to go to Budapest. And even if the Hungarians did listen in on us last night, what I do in private even with a diplomat isn't any concern of theirs. Nor of the British Council's, for that matter. I'm over twenty-one."

"Be that as it may, if I were to be accused of involvement in activities prejudicial to the Hungarian state it might go hard with you too, now that they probably know that we're, well – "

"Fucking each other? Go on, say it, Ben. Now you listen to me. I don't know what you take me for, but think, I'm a reasonably intelligent woman. And although I don't know exactly what all this is about or why you never saw fit to mention this little matter of the lorry before, I do know a set-up when I see one. I've been thinking, and in my opinion that bloke with the cart was one of Agnes and Sandor's uncles."

Lazenby breathed in sharply, taken aback. "You think that, do you?"

"Yes I do. That mysterious rendezvous at Hortobagy was just a ploy to get you here this evening. The gipsies are obviously returning your lorryload of paintings to you out of gratitude for Gosta Lundin's sympathy and help. And yours too, you fathead. And even left the truck pointing the right way. I don't see how it can possibly be 'prejudicial to the Hungarian state' as you so pompously put it if you take delivery of what's yours anyway. All you have to do is drive the thing back to Budapest. Unless you want me to."

"For God's sake, don't be ridiculous."

"Nothing ridiculous about it. It's bound to have power-assisted steering. Come on, let's have a look." Whereupon the surprising Emma Jarvis opened the door of the Rover, tripped lightly over to the huge truck and swarmed up and into the cab as if to the manner born.

Stunned, Lazenby joined her from the other side of the cab, which was similarly equipped with footholds and a hand grip. Its door was also unlocked. His ascent was even more ungainly than before and he contrived to jacknife his body over the doorsill, having to haul himself the rest of the way with his arms, wincing in pain.

"Oopsadaisy! You're out of condition, Lazenby." Emma grinned at him cheerfully, and turned the ignition key half-way so that the instrument panel lit up. "Jolly nice rig, this," she said. "It's my guess that they'll have filled the tank for us. I'll just start her up and check the fuel gauge." She turned the key, and the powerful diesel engine fired at once. Emma briefly revved it, then switched off, to Lazenby's enormous relief.

"Yup. Plenty of diesel. Oil gauge fine, too."

"Emma, this is quite insane!"

"You have a better idea?"

"But where? . . . How? I mean – "

"How come a nicely brought up doctor of philosophy knows how to handle an articulated lorry? Well, I'm *not going to tell you*. That information is on a need to know basis. Suffice it that once I've changed into the flat-heeled shoes I have in my bag I'm quite capable of driving this little lady to Budapest. Are you?"

"Well, I . . ."

"That's settled, then. If you'd wanted to have a go I'd have volunteered to follow you in the Rover, but I think that might indeed upset the fuzz. Whereas if you follow me and we're stopped, you can explain to them that you've recovered stolen British Embassy property and are escorting it back to where it belongs."

"OK, you seem to know what you're doing, but how the hell am I supposed to justify letting you drive a commercial vehicle, may I ask? Everybody you pass would have a fit to see a young woman up here in the driver's seat."

"You're quite wrong about that, you know. If you come across a big truck like this on the road, do you honestly look to see who's driving it? Besides, you've explained to me ad nauseam that your own car's madly conspicuous and that every policeman who spots you will whip out his little notebook and make a report. They won't even notice me, I promise you. And in any case as it happens I have my international driving permit in my bag. And it's valid for heavy goods vehicles too, I'll have you know."

Lazenby groaned. Ten minutes later, after arguing with and losing to an obstinately nonchalant and newly assertive Emma, he was at the wheel of the Rover again, having made a three-point turn so as to face in the direction of Budapest. He was far from happy. Emma's hypothesis had its merits, but she was completely wrong about the Hortobagy connection, and he now wished he'd confessed to having lied to her about the timing of the rendezvous.

It was hardly credible that even if the gipsies were behind all this they would have risked leaving the lorry there in daylight. It was all a horrible mess.

In spite of his deep misgivings it was with something approaching awe that Lazenby watched Emma as she confidently walked in her flat-heeled shoes from end to end of Ivan's juggernaut, studying the amount of clearance available for her to extricate it from the lean-to without damage to either. Then she returned to the cab and lithely clambered up into it, incongruous in her short skirt. Lazenby heard the roar of the engine and saw the lights blaze out, then the driver's window was lowered and he saw the grin on her small face as she gave him a thumbs-up sign.

It was quite beautiful to watch. The great vehicle snaked out of its berth with elegant grace and gathered speed until it was cruising along rock-steady at a sedate sixty kilometres an hour, with Lazenby trailing it a hundred metres behind.

"He's made pretty good time," the AVH liaison man at traffic police headquarters in Budapest said on the phone to his headquarters after the report came in from the policeman on duty at the junction of the Szolnok road with the airport approach road. Nobody had told him to keep an eye open for articulated lorries, but he had spotted a snazzy green car with diplomatic plates heading into the city, and dutifully noted its registration number. The AVH man had checked it against his list for form's sake: it was Lazenby all right, logged out with a woman passenger but returning on his own. "No respect for speed limits."

The man at the other end shrugged. "Diplomats are like that. The buggers have charmed lives, but there's no need to get excited about it." He rang off. Since the Englishman was going to be on his own there was no fun to be had out of activating the bugs at his house tonight.

Lazenby pulled ahead of the lorry when they were well into the city proper, as Emma had asked him to do, in order to pilot her to Heroes' Square and the art gallery. The fact that neither the lorry nor his own car had been challenged on the way had done little to calm his jangling nerves. All right, Emma had driven the damn thing like a professional, but assuming they covered the last mile or two without being stopped and arrived safely at the gallery, what then? It was after eleven, and the place would undoubtedly be locked up like a drum. There'd presumably be a night security man around somewhere, but he could hardly be expected to accept responsibility for the paintings; and however sinister its connections, the KKI switchboard closed down every evening at five-thirty sharp.

He entered Heroes' Square still worrying over the problem, swung round to the back of the great black bulk of the museum with Emma following, and pulled up in the parking area. He hardly noticed the expert way she manoeuvred the lorry, backing it up so that its rear doors were neatly aligned with the concertina gates of the service entrance. Silence fell as she switched off first the engine and then the air conditioning, and within a few seconds she had descended from her high perch in the cab, run the few yards to the Rover and slipped into its passenger seat.

"May I suggest that we should make ourselves scarce?" she asked politely. "I've brought the ignition keys, so nobody's going to nick it all that easily."

They hadn't discussed the subject, but it was plain to Lazenby that for good or ill he had to abandon any thought of taking Emma anywhere but to his house.

He was physically and mentally exhausted, and like an automaton reached out to switch on the engine again.

"Ben, there's somebody coming!"

"Night security guard, I expect," Lazenby mumbled, and rolled his window down. "I'll tell him to keep an eye on the lorry until the staff turn up tomorrow morning."

He sat there dully, watching the dark figure of a man approach, but jerked into full consciousness when he spoke not to himself but to Emma, in confident English. "Well done, Miss Jarvis. You are a most accomplished driver. And Mr Lazenby, please be assured that the paintings will be quite safe here overnight, and will be 'found' by the museum authorities in the morning. You must be very tired, but my friends and I hope very much that you will come to Hortobagy tomorrow morning at eleven as originally planned, and bring Miss Jarvis with you. Agnes and Sandor will be there to greet you, and we have some entertainment planned for you. Goodnight to you both. Sleep well."

Chapter Twenty-Three

Lazenby managed to swing his legs over the edge of the bed and assume a slumped sitting position, but had to remain in it for some time before he felt confident enough to attempt to walk. When eventually he did, he blinked and eyed the distance – about three yards – between him and the window, then bravely lurched over to it and saw that the sky was blue and already high enough for its rays to touch the roofs of the houses on the other side of the street. It was Saturday, and seven-twenty by the watch which was all he had on.

He turned and surveyed with bleary appreciation the equally naked top half of Emma Jarvis, who was lying on her side with the sheet down to her hip. She looked just as innocently delightful as she had done when welcoming him to her bath on Thursday evening, but since then she had shown herself to be so much more than that. For a start, she was an expert driver with an HGV licence. Second, she had demonstrated a resourcefulness and decisiveness Lazenby was painfully conscious he lacked, and had been willing to risk great deal more than he had. Good grief, and *she* thought *he* was a spy!

He returned to the bedside, reached out and applied gentle pressure to her shoulder. "Time to get up, my love," he said. Emma woke at once, blinked a few times and then smiled.

"The worst thing about you is that you keep making me get up before I want to," she said. "Beast. Sadist."

Then she made for the second bathroom and Lazenby retired to his own, took a shower, shaved and dressed while he thought back over the extraordinary events of the past few days, culminating in the weird encounter with the well-spoken gipsy behind the art museum. Even that seemed to have left Emma totally unfazed, and she'd chattered away happily while they were driving back to the house, eaten an omelette she cooked, and tumbled into bed together.

Lazenby shook his head indulgently, and then froze in his tracks, his fingers motionless in the middle of buttoning up his shirt as yet another disconcerting idea struck him. Christ almighty, suppose it was *Emma* who was the spy! He finished dressing in something of a daze and made his way to the kitchen to make some coffee. Emma reappeared after a while very lightly made-up and dressed unobtrusively in jeans and a loose T-shirt, and carrying the small soft-topped suitcase which was all the luggage she had brought with her from Debrecen. She yawned mightily, then grinned at Lazenby, came over to him and gave him a brief hug.

"Hello, lover. Too tired, he said. Hah! Let me at that coffee."

He returned the hug and tried to behave as normally as his state of mind permitted, even to the extent of murmuring as they went downstairs that they should perhaps stick to banalities while in the car, which for want of a garage at the house had to be parked in the street, where it could easily be tampered with. Since it would be impossible to conceal their destination, he took along a guide book which Emma studied; and they discussed the tourist delights of the national park at Hortobagy and exclaimed pointedly about the suitability of the weather for a detour to see it before going on to Debrecen.

It was at a little before ten that they came to the lean-to shed where the lorry had been waiting the previous evening, adrift as it were like the Marie Celeste. Lazenby slowed down as they passed, and Emma put out a hand to squeeze his, but neither spoke until they reached the T-junction at Kenderes. There she looked up from the map and reminded him to turn left, for that was the recommended tourist route which would bring them to Hortobagy. There was even less traffic than there had been on the main road, and they made good time.

"There it is, Ben! The longest stone road bridge in Hungary."

"So it is. Thank you, Miss Baedeker."

Lazenby glanced across at Emma, still wondering about her, and drove slowly over the renowned Nine-Arch Bridge across the Hortobagy River. It was as if he and Emma were alone in a deserted landscape. There was no sign of Agnes or Sandor, nor indeed of any other living soul.

"Well, here we are, sort of. It's ten forty-five," he said. "I wonder what we should do?"

"It's less than a mile to Mata, where the guided tours start from. The guidebook says it's very busy there at this time of the year. So why don't we go there? You never know," Emma added slyly, "you might easily bump into somebody you know."

Colonel Galitsin sat in the back of one of the KGB's unmarked cars – a BMW with Hungarian hire-car plates – scowling at the two people in the front seats. He would have felt much safer in an official Soviet Embassy vehicle, but had to accept that if they were to pass for foreign tourists a certain amount of protective coloration was necessary. It was one thing to travel with the KGB Deputy Resident, however, but quite another to accept that his assistant the lieutenant had been pressed into service as chauffeur, and quite outrageous that Svetlana Ivanova had elected to sit beside him in the front passenger seat.

She was wearing designer jeans and an oversized sweater, and sported fashionable sun-glasses: an outfit that the Colonel admitted to himself did make her look like a well-heeled western tourist. The lieutenant too had dressed appropriately, in a sporty polo shirt and well-cut trousers, but the Colonel was conscious of the fact that, even though he was himself in civilian clothes and had gone so far as to leave his necktie behind, his cropped hair and stiffly military demeanour made it unlikely that he could be taken for anything other than a Russian officer.

They were about half way to Hortobagy, and Colonel Galitsin noted with mounting distaste that, while the lieutenant's head was necessarily in much the same position as it had been earlier, that of Svetlana Ivanova had shifted several inches nearer to it. That she was, not to put too fine a point on it, snuggling up to the young man, who was driving with only his right hand on the wheel. Galitsin leaned well forward in his seat and was able to confirm his suspicions by catching a glimpse of of a well-manicured KGB hand resting on a Soviet Army thigh and vice versa before he cleared his throat thunderously and they were at once withdrawn. Svetlana Ivanova turned in her seat and looked coolly at Galitsin.

"Yes, Colonel?"

"You did say you have arranged for some back-up?"

"I did. Two members of my staff have gone ahead and will base themselves at the rest house in Hortobagy village. And you?"

"I spoke to my cousin Major Vishinski. He will be in the vicinity with three picked men, um, road-testing an armoured car."

"A *what*? I suggested a *discreet* Soviet Army presence, not a show of force!"

Galitsin *had* thus far deferred to his KGB colleague even though they were technically of equal rank. He knew that when push came to shove, a KGB colonel wielded very much more power than his or in this case her military counterpart. Within the Soviet Embassy Svetlana Ivanova and her boss effectively outranked everybody else, not excluding the Ambassador himself. All the same, the Soviet Army had a good many divisions stationed in Hungary, and he was hanged if he was going to be lectured on professional matters by a tart who was enjoying being groped by his own assistant.

"You look after your business, Comrade, and I'll look after mine," he snapped, wishing he could have thought up a more effective retort.

"I certainly don't intend to let your relation interfere with my surveillance operation, I can assure you. I just hope the AVH doesn't misinterpret the situation, that's all. It's obvious they'll be around as well." She flounced round in her seat and faced forward again.

"I'm not cross with *you*, Lieutenant," Galitsin heard her croon after a while. "And I think you drive beautifully. Mm, go on, that feels nice."

The brazen hussy.

Chapter Twenty-Four

If the cluster of buildings that comprised Mata could be said to have a focal point, it was an extensive range of stables. Beside them was a cafe already full of customers chattering in a variety of languages, with an overspill of groups of two and three standing about outside drinking coffee and watching the bustle as horses were led out by men and boys and harnessed to a number of covered wagons. An agreeable commingling of the smells of horse manure, hay, coffee and cigarette smoke pervaded the air, and there was a general atmosphere of pleasurable excitement.

Most of the stable hands wore nondescript clothing, but some of the men were tricked out in elaborate if sweat-soiled and dusty traditional finery. Colourfully embroidered open waistcoats set off smocked linen shirts with full sleeves buttoned at the wrist, and baggy, plain black trousers were tucked into high boots. Waiting by the wagons were even more splendid figures: tall, fiercely moustachioed men in round hats, blue or white shirts and divided skirts terminating well below the tops of their boots.

"The ones in the doggy-bowl hats and the trendy culottes must be the drivers, wouldn't you think?" Lazenby said as they stood beside the car, which he had parked temporarily beside one Austrian and two West German-registered tour buses and about a dozen other cars. Two of the latter also bore Austrian plates, while one had blue diplomatic ones, similar to the ones on Lazenby's Rover. Its registration number identified it as belonging to a member of the French Embassy. Emma still had the guidebook in her hand and consulted it briefly. "I expect so. The horses," she went on to announce, "are of the prize-winning Noniusz breed."

"Wow," Lazenby said absently. "Fancy that." He was experiencing what he decided was a kind of constipation of the mental processes, and perhaps for that reason was quite enjoying himself watching the horses and their grooms and presumed riders, one of whom was approaching with a friendly smile.

"Lazenby-*Ur*? *Madame*? I kiss your hand," he said in Hungarian, suiting action to words by seizing Emma's and raising it to within an inch of his moustache, but sparing Lazenby. He produced two slips of paper from the recesses of his voluminous divided skirt. "Here are your tickets. You ride with me." He indicated the nearest wagon. "Come, please."

They exchanged uncertain looks and the man's manner became more pressing. He lowered his voice. "I am the uncle of Sandor and Agnes. Please come with me." Then he bowed to them both with theatrical extravagance and backed away, beckoning. Smiling timidly, Emma began to move towards the wagon and Lazenby followed suit.

Each of the several wagons had a small wheeled flight of three or four shallow steps placed behind it: they looked like miniature wooden versions of the ones used at small airports. A general movement of sightseers to the wagons had begun, and the first had already moved off with a great creaking of iron-tyred wooden wheels, snorting of horses, hallooing and cracking of whips, and jingling of harness. It looked to Lazenby as if about twenty passengers were being helped into each cart, and his apprehensiveness increased when he realised that no others were being directed to the one he and Emma were being urged to board.

Emma went first up the steps, but recoiled with a badly suppressed scream before she reached the top. Hastening to her, Lazenby soon saw the reason. There were already about a dozen people occupying the bench seats inside, and not one of them looked remotely like a tourist. Though it was rolled up at either side to a height of about eighteen inches, the thick canvas hood cut out all the sunshine and filled the interior with greenish gloom, making the vehicle and its shabbily dressed denizens look like a den of thieves as depicted by a Victorian book illustrator. It was with small surprise that Lazenby discerned the seemingly undernourished but nevertheless wiry forms of Agnes and her younger brother among the company within.

"Quick, boss, missis. These my uncles. They help." For all the urgency in her tone, Agnes was every bit the accomplished hostess, offering introductions all round amid a ragged chorus of greetings from the men inside. All, with the obvious exception of Sandor, seemed to be between about twenty and forty years of age, and each shook Lazenby warmly by the hand and greeted Emma with clumsy gallantry.

One of the men produced and dusted off a couple of flat cushions for the newcomers, and another offered them a swig from one of several bottles of apricot brandy that were circulating. Emma declined with an apologetic little smile, and Lazenby only pretended to drink, with his thumb firmly over the aperture. Then he looked round and asked in English if anybody could please explain what was going on. After a few seconds one of the men was shoved forward by his immediate neighbours. His moustache was particularly shaggy, and his eyes glittered in the shadows, but when he spoke it was in a pleasingly modulated tenor.

"Yes. I am Ferencz Molnar. It was my brother Istvan who greeted you at the art museum in Budapest last night.

I too speak some English, but not as well as Istvan. I must begin by apologising to you for the manner in which you have been invited here. Agnes referred to us as her uncles, but she uses the term loosely – oops!" The incongruously ladylike expletive was occasioned by a shuddering lurch as their cart began to move, which made him and several others sway on their benches and led to some spillage from the bottle of *palinka* Molnar was holding. He smiled sweetly before continuing in the same schoolmasterly style as before.

"We are all related in some way to Agnes and Sandor, but are mostly cousins. And some of us have been assisting and protecting them throughout their travels during the past week."

"Go on," Lazenby said, and took Emma's free hand in his and squeezed it. They needed one each to clutch at the bench as their cart swayed and jolted over the rutted track. "Am I to understand that it wasn't on their own initiative that they followed me to Romania, then?"

Molnar glanced affectionately at the children, who were sitting huddled together and paradoxically seemed more vulnerable now that they were among friends and allies. "No, but they have shown much resourcefulness during this affair, and we are very proud of both of them."

"So you should be proud of them," Emma cut in. "They're terrific."

"You speak of 'this affair'. I think you owe us an explanation," Lazenby said, brusquely interrupting the flow of compliments.

"Yes, we do. You will have gathered that we maintain extensive links with our brothers and sisters in the territory under Romanian control, and we have ways and means of exchanging information. We frequently visit each other, in point of fact. So we know all about the madman Ceauşescu's murderous plans for our people, and the efforts of courageous dissidents – including one or two informants among his own immediate entourage – to frustrate them. We also learned that the journalist Gosta Lundin had been given an opportunity to interview him, and that a tape recording had been made of remarks of Ceauşescu's which would utterly discredit him if used in the right way. That tape was, as I think you know, passed to Gosta Lundin, whom we know to be sympathetic to the plight of our people."

"All right, I accept all that. But what I don't understand is this. You've boasted about the efficiency of your intelligence network and the fact that you can go to and fro across the frontier more or less at will. Therefore your people could obviously have spirited the tape out of Romania without involving Gosta, or me, or Dr Jarvis here."

"Yes, Mr Lazenby, we could have done that, but what notice would anyone have taken of material produced by ourselves, Ceauşescu's intended victims? Except to denounce it as an obvious fake? Whereas Gosta Lundin is an unimpeachably objective and internationally respected journalist. When she reveals the contents of the tape and the true story of how much she and others risked to smuggle it out of Romania, we shall have world opinion on our side."

"You're very persuasive, Mr Molnar. And you and your brother speak remarkably good English."

"You're wary of me, Mr Lazenby. And justifiably so. Istvan and I are political activists involved in an international problem, so we've made it our business to learn the kind of English we need to persuade people like yourself to pay attention to what we say."

Lazenby met his level gaze. "Very well, convince me of your good faith by giving me straight answers to three questions." He let go of Emma's hand in order to hold up three fingers which he crooked one by one as he continued. "First, what do you know about the arrest of

Gosta Lundin by the AVH yesterday morning? Second, where is this famous tape recording now? And third, what was the meaning of your games with the Bulgarian truck? It was you who hijacked it, I assume?"

Molnar nodded his acknowledgement of the questions and went into a huddle with the two or three of his companions who appeared to be in authority over the others. Lazenby found it quite impossible to comprehend even the general import of their discussion, conducted as it was in undertones, and in rapid and idiomatic Hungarian. After a short while Molnar spoke directly to Emma and Lazenby again.

"The third of your questions is easy to answer. We had you under observation throughout your journey, and seized a wonderful opportunity which presented itself to us at Kecskemet to make off with one of the trucks in order to confuse the Hungarian authorities. We concealed it for a little over twenty-four hours and restored it to you yesterday evening. It may reassure you to know that the driver came to no physical harm and that the crates inside the truck were not tampered with in any way."

Molnar looked at a huge old-fashioned pocket watch that he produced from his waistcoat. "By now they are safely in the custody of the museum authorities. Your second question concerned the tape recording. It is in the hands of the Finnish Ambassador, who learned of Gosta Lundin's abduction promptly thanks to you, Mr Lazenby, and is negotiating her release. As to why the AVH took her into custody, I can only guess, and your guess is as good as mine." Molnar shrugged, and leaned across to listen to a muttered remark from one of the other men.

"We hope to stage something memorable later on, but the regular programme is about to begin, so for the present please try to enjoy it and behave as much like ordinary tourists as possible," he then said, before turning again to his friends. Lazenby looked at Emma.

"Do you feel like an ordinary tourist, Emma?"

"No. I feel as if I'm in a Hollywood film. Those sheep over there are very Disneyland, don't you think? This seems to be one of those situations where the only thing to do is to lie back and think of England." She smiled, reached for Lazenby's hand again and ran a thoughtful forefinger over his palm, lowering her voice. "Incidentally, I wouldn't like you to get the idea that I devoted any thought to England last night. Or the night before."

In the forty-five minutes that followed, their wagon trundled over the grassy prairie making several stops, and Lazenby found himself admiring the skill with which their driver contrived to keep them at a distance from the several other carts making the circuit at the same time, and neatly positioned his wagon whenever they stopped so that only its back, with Lazenby and Emma prominently displayed, was visible to the other tourists.

At each halt they were treated to a different display. Herds of sheep with horns twisted like old-fashioned barley sugar, water buffalo, wild boar and peculiar looking cattle, were each in turn rounded up and brought within convenient viewing distance of the spectators by an assortment of specialist herdsmen with the assistance of sheepdogs that looked like animated shagpile rugs, and from time to time bareback stunt riders thundered past standing straddled across two horses while controlling another three with long reins.

"It really is quite interesting, I must admit," Lazenby said after a particularly close pass by one of the horsemen, who found time to shout something to their own driver who immediately dragged at the reins on one side and set a new course, away from the other wagons, and cracked his long whip until they were careering at speed. Lazenby and Emma clutched at each other to keep their balance, and became aware of Sandor and Agnes at their side, dancing in gleeful excitement.

"We have fun now, Missis, Boss! Don' worry, my uncles fix bastards!"

Lazenby couldn't imagine what Agnes meant, but then sat bolt upright, rubbed his eyes and stared hard. "Good lord, look who's here! No, over there, to the left. I'm willing to swear that's Dracula's car at the back."

Emma peered in the direction he was pointing. "No! I can't *believe* it!" In the distance, bumping across the grass, was a strange little procession of motor vehicles, led by what in his excitement Lazenby at first took to be a tank, but after a moment realised was an armoured car with military markings. Lurching and swaying behind it were two ordinary cars, and bringing up the rear was the bloated black Chaika limousine from the KKI. The newcomers were coming towards them diagonally, and to judge from their speed over the rough terrain were, with the exception of the armoured car, doing expensive damage to their suspensions.

"Well, they're bound to catch us up before long. I hope our friends were expecting visitors."

"Oh yes, Mr Lazenby, we were. And we are quite ready for them." It was Molnar, looking quite animated.

"Who on earth are they, Mr Molnar?" Emma enquired. "We think we recognise the black car at the back, but . . ."

"The lead vehicle is a Russian armoured car. It has been patrolling the area since very early this morning. The one at the back which you think you recognise is a car belonging to the KKI, driven by an AVH man called Nagy with a genuine KKI official as passenger. His name is believed to be Szekacs."

"Well, we know him all right. We call him Dracula, don't we, Ben?"

"Viktor Szekacs is responsible for the safe delivery of

the consignment of paintings in the truck you hijacked," Lazenby said cautiously. "He must have got hold of the idea that you're taking us to it."

"He has. We arranged for him to be given certain misleading information as soon as he arrived at Mata, on the assumption that his AVH companion would make sure that other interested parties were advised. That will be the people in the other two cars. None of them know as yet that the paintings have been returned to Budapest. Anyway, a diversion has been arranged . . . ah, here they come."

Even above the creaking and screech of the ill-lubricated wheels of their wagon and the jingling of harness, snorting of horses and whipcracking and shouts from their driver, they could hear the thunder of hooves in the distance, and before long they could see what looked like a stampede of several dozen unbroken young horses rapidly closing on the column of vehicles.

"Gee, it's the US Cavalry," Lazenby murmured as he spotted the outriders controlling the direction of the wild rush and urging the horses on. Their menacing approach must have seemed terrifying to the drivers of the cars, and even affected the nerves of the soldier driving the Russian armoured car, because he veered away and the others followed. The men directing the horses expertly wheeled their charges round and the pursuers became the pursued, fleeing from the dense phalanx of excited animals.

"What's in that direction?" Lazenby enquired.

Molnar smiled. "We're going to show you," he said as their wagon changed course once more and set out to follow the horses. "Look ahead if you can, from the left side."

There wasn't far to go, and they soon reached the reed-fringed bank of the Great Fish Pond. From this vantage point they witnessed the humiliation of Major Vishinski stranded in his armoured car, and saw the KGB Deputy Resident being carried to dry land by her tall young lieutenant, while Colonel Galitsin floundered in their wake, along with an assortment of AVH men including a bellowing Comrade Nagy with drenched trouser-legs. Last of all came Viktor Szekacs. For all four vehicles had been deftly herded into two feet of water over a bed of soft mud into which they were slowly but steadily sinking. In the confusion, Lazenby murmured into Emma's ear.

"I say, Emma, are you a spy, by any chance?"

"Ben, don't be so daft! Whatever made you think that?"

"Just wondering. Tell me this, then. Who taught you to drive a lorry? I really need to know."

"Ah. Well, Agnes and Sandor aren't the only ones with useful uncles. Mine runs a haulage business. In Basingstoke. You'll find it in the yellow pages. By the way, are you married?"

"I used to be, but I'm not now."

"Ah. And do you fancy Gosta Lundin?"

"Good lord, no. I wouldn't go to bed with her even if she offered. Not now."

Chapter Twenty-Five

It was eleven in the morning, not the best time to hold a reception; but the Director of the National Fine Art Gallery had insisted on holding the formal opening ceremony at that time. It was performed jointly by the Hungarian Minister of Culture and Her Britannic Majesty's Ambassador. An unusually large number of people were present at what was after all a routine occasion, and this was in all probability due more to the promise of the *vin d'honneur* referred to on the invitation cards than to the solid worth of the paintings. To Lazenby, though, it was as if the ranks of Tuscany had turned out to cheer. Of course, he reflected, a number of gate-crashers had put in an appearance in order to find out if there was any truth in the rumours flying around town.

Dracula was there *ex officio*, as was his director and the secretary he meekly lusted after. Lazenby couldn't see Comrade Nagy, but had no doubt that he was lurking somewhere in the vicinity. The rather dashing lady of a certain age he had seen being rescued from the Great Fish Pond at Hortobagy by a young man he presumed to be her toy-boy was there, as was a Soviet military officer in uniform: a very rare sight in Budapest. Lazenby briefly wondered why their hats had to be so enormous. Then there were two men in narrow suits and button-down collars with what Lazenby recognised as CIA haircuts: he wondered why they hadn't shown up at an earlier stage in the saga.

Needless to say, there was a good turn-out of members of Hungary's licensed intelligentsia: he waved at bluff old Ivan Boldizsar of the Writers' Union, whose name he had given to the communist garage man in Szolnok, and greeted several other acquaintances including the stylish blonde widow of the composer Kodaly. All the beautiful people of Budapest had turned up in spite of the early hour: surely they couldn't all have heard about the Hortobagy fiasco or seen the photographs that Ferencz Molnar had taken unnoticed before his accomplices "volunteered" to help dislodge the waterlogged vehicles from their watery resting place. Lazenby had been given a set which he would treasure.

It was such a shame that Emma couldn't be there: they'd exchanged fond farewells in the Rover outside her apartment block in Debrecen. That had been after the show was over and they'd had lunch in Mata with Agnes and Sandor as the guests of Ferencz Molnar and a few more of the "uncles". They'd parted good friends with the gipsies, and with each other; and he knew he would see Emma again before long. It was just as well on the whole: had she had been at the reception he would have had to introduce her to Gosta Lundin, who might have said something ambiguous about their perfectly proper dinner together the previous evening.

"Gosta, come and say hello to my boss . . . Ambassador, I'd like you to meet Gosta Lundin. Ms Lundin is a distinguished journalist from Finland. You'll remember I told you she was very helpful in connection with transporting some of the paintings from Bucharest."

"Indeed I remember. Good morning, Miss Lundin. Pleasure to meet you." The British Ambassador hung on to Gosta's hand rather longer than strict protocol required, but Lazenby was sympathetic. She looked stunning in a dull green silk suit which she must surely have borrowed from one of her Scandinavian friends. "What d'you think of our paintings?"

"Good morning, Your Excellency. Congratulations. They're very . . . impressive. I saw them when they were displayed in Bucharest, of course. Unlikely to offend, I think."

The Ambassador released her hand with obvious regret and roared with professional laughter. "My word, yes, and that's a consideration, especially in this part of the world. I don't mind telling you I was a bit worried when Lazenby here told me the British Council was laying on an exhibition. You never know what they're going to get up to next, you see. Thought they might send some of that stuff with swear words all over it, or – "

Lazenby cut in. "Or a stripper writhing about?"

"Extraordinary you should say that, Ben. Months ago my opposite number in Bucharest and I ran across each other in London and I mentioned that I'd heard we'd both be getting an exhibition about now. He told me the most peculiar story about . . . oh well, we mustn't embarrass Miss Lundin here." Far from seeming embarrassed, Gosta snorted inelegantly with laughter.

"You mean Cosy Fanny Tutti," she spluttered at last. "Ben told me about her last night."

"Last night?"

"Yes. We had dinner together. Didn't we, Ben?"

The Ambassador harrumphed, almost but not quite sure that he was being made a fool of, but decided not to be offended. "Anyway, all's well that ends well, eh? Oh, here's my Finnish colleague coming over. Felt I should invite him to the opening specially, in view of, er . . ."

"Congratulations on the exhibition, Malcolm," the Finnish Ambassador said to his confrere as he joined them, hand outstretched. "Damn fine show." He smiled at the other two. "Good morning, both of you. You're looking well after your various experiences, I must say."

He turned again to the British Ambassador. "I've told you this already, Malcolm, but I do want to say again how grateful we are to Mr Lazenby for all the help he gave to Gosta Lundin. It can't have been easy for him, but he followed all the twists and turns with great skill and resourcefulness. And it was thanks to his friends that I was supplied with the very amusing photographs that I used to, well, persuade the authorities that they must release Miss Lundin forthwith." He smiled broadly, stifling a most undiplomatic snigger. "And what's more, Gosta tells me that she may be able to acquire the negatives, which might be of great value to us Finns in future negotiations with our Soviet neighbours, who don't like being made to look fools. I'm not really being indiscreet, because your Mr Lazenby will have told you all about them anyway."

"Yes. There seems to be no limit to Lazenby's passion for pictures of one sort and another," the British Ambassador said drily.

"Quite so. It was very stupid of the AVH to imagine that she knew the whereabouts of the missing truck anyway. It seems that some idiot decided to mount a little operation of his own and target Miss Lundin in what the Ministry of Foreign Affairs described to me as an excess of zeal. I was told in confidence that he ordered her arrest on his own initiative on the basis of information received from a personal contact in Arad."

"Ha! It had to be. Comrade Nagy strikes again," Lazenby said, and immediately wished he hadn't.

"Who?"

"Oh, er, nothing really, Ambassador. 'Comrade Nagy' is just my generic name for any Hungarian official who cocks things up."

"I'm bound to say I don't think that's terribly funny, Ben. However, in the circumstances . . ." The Ambassador turned back to his Finnish colleague. "Well, thank you for being so forthcoming, Jan. And I'll make sure your kind words about Ben Lazenby are passed on to the British Council in London." The Ambassador turned to Gosta. "Delightful meeting you, Miss Lundin. I wonder if you'd care to come to lunch with me some time? I'll get in touch."